Valentine Flings

An affair to mend their broken hearts?

When nurse Ally signs herself and her best friend,
GP Larissa, up for a posting with global charity
New Health Frontiers, the idea is that they both
see a bit of the world and hopefully find a little
fun along the way!

After all, both women are nursing heartbreaks that
have held them back from embracing life to the
fullest, and as their assignments will put them in
some far-flung locations at the most romantic time of
the year, they decide to up the ante and dare each
other to embark on a no-strings affair while away!

But they both find much more than they were
expecting when their flings have the potential to turn
from a bit of fun into happily-ever-after...

Indulge in Larissa and Erik's story in
Hot Nights with the Arctic Doc by Luana DaRosa

And fall for Ally and Dev in
Nurse's Keralan Temptation by Becky Wicks

Both available now!

T0284517

Dear Reader,

Thank you for picking up *Hot Nights with the Arctic Doc*, the first book in the Valentine Flings duet.

I have to say I have rarely had so much fun writing a book. This one definitely ranks as one of my favourites. The setting was so much fun to explore, especially from a medical perspective. Because Svalbard is so isolated, there are only so many things one can do, but all of them are rather unique. And then there is Erik, who feels so indebted to his community that he grew up in, while Larissa is on the opposite side of the spectrum, having lived a life unrooted until she met her best friend, Ally. So when she's suddenly thrown into this very intimate, close-knit group, it challenges many of the beliefs she's always held.

Speaking of Ally, I do hope you will also check out her story, *Nurse's Keralan Temptation* by my dear friend Becky Wicks. We've spent many hours on the phone hiding little Easter eggs here and there throughout the story, and I can't wait for all of you to discover them.

Happy reading!

Luana <3

HOT NIGHTS WITH THE ARCTIC DOC

LUANA DaROSA

MEDICAL ROMANCE

Harlequin®
MEDICAL
ROMANCE

ISBN-13: 978-1-335-94280-7

Hot Nights with the Arctic Doc

Copyright © 2025 by Luana DaRosa

Recycling programs for this product may not exist in your area.

Harlequin Enterprises ULC
22 Adelaide St. West, 41st Floor
Toronto, Ontario M5H 4E3, Canada
www.Harlequin.com

Printed in U.S.A.

Once at home in sunny Brazil, **Luana DaRosa** has since lived on three different continents, though her favorite romantic location remains the tropical places of Latin America. When she's not typing away at her latest romance novel or reading about love, Luana is either crocheting, buying yarn she doesn't need or chasing her bunnies around her house. She lives with her partner in a cozy town in the south of England. Find her on X under the handle @ludarosabooks.

Books by Luana DaRosa

Harlequin Medical Romance

Amazon River Vets

The Vet's Convenient Bride
The Secret She Kept from Dr. Delgado

Buenos Aires Docs

Surgeon's Brooding Brazilian Rival

Falling for Her Off-Limits Boss
Her Secret Rio Baby
Falling Again for the Brazilian Doc
A Therapy Pup to Reunite Them
Pregnancy Surprise with the Greek Surgeon

Visit the Author Profile page at Harlequin.com.

For Becky—the first of hopefully many!

PROLOGUE

'HEY, CHECK THIS OUT.' The voice of Larissa's best friend, Ally, barely registered as she took a sip from her coffee, wincing at the taste. Considering a three-day-old muffin that had, on a previous visit, chipped her tooth and the porcelain dolls sitting on floating shelves along the wall, Larissa had no idea why Heaton Perk was their favourite coffee shop. Neither of them were particularly into regular dental emergencies or creepy dolls whose eyes followed you around no matter where you sat.

Ally nudged her knee under the table, bringing her attention back to the tablet in front of them. 'Larry, we have to make a plan.'

'Okay, for the last time—Larry is a name for a cat,' Larissa said, taking another sip of coffee that landed like cement in the bottom of her stomach.

Ally's lips parted in a sheepish grin, and she gave Larissa's knee another shove. 'And I told you this way our names sound like a pair. Larry and Ally! You are always so serious—unless I want to talk about the future.'

Larissa groaned, her head coming down onto the rickety table. 'Because I'm still in denial about our practice closing. We built this for the last five years, pouring endless hours and care into it. Now suddenly the trust decides that this community doesn't need our services anymore?'

They'd both woken up last week to the news that their clinic had lost its funding and would shut down at the end of the year. What a great way to celebrate Christmas—finding a new place to work when she'd just got comfortable down here in Frome, in the south of England. For someone like her, who preferred solitude and self-sufficiency above anything else, five years seemed like a fast timeline to get comfortable, if she was being honest.

Now, they would spend the rest of the month updating their patients on this recent development and then get all of their documentation in order so they could transfer things to the GP clinic in a different district.

Ally's face grew serious. 'I'm right there with you—it sucks. But we have to…move on.'

Larissa lifted her head at that, noticing the hesitation in her last words. Were they meant for her or Ally herself? God knew they both had their fair share of baggage they carried around.

'What if I don't want to work in a place without you?' she said, steering the conversation away from where she could see the clouds building. 'There's no Dr Costa without Nurse Spencer.'

Larissa almost sighed when the sheepish grin returned to the other woman's face. She tapped on the tablet again, drawing Larissa's attention to it. 'I thought about that, and I have a solution.'

Looking at the screen, Larissa narrowed her eyes. 'New Health Frontiers?'

'It's a non profit organisation that matches medical professionals with places who need their certain skills. There are tons of places looking for short-term GPs and nurses. What if we take this entire mess with the clinic and with Rachel—' Larissa couldn't stop the wince at the sound of her ex-girlfriend's name '—and my long overdue return to the dating pool…and go on an adventure?'

When her best friend looked at her with bright eyes, Larissa remained unconvinced. 'An adventure?'

'Yes, Larry. A solo adventure for each of us. It'll get us both out of this place and give us some distance—we'll gain some perspective. Plus, while we are away, we can message and call to make our plan about what to do next. Because in the long term, I don't want to work without you, either.'

Larissa looked down at the murky coffee, thinking it must have been extra-old, because somehow Ally was making sense with this proposal. Without work keeping her anchored, Larissa didn't know what to do with herself. Had nothing tying her down, occupying space inside her that, if left empty, would send her thoughts down a spiral. Work was how she kept her independence. Without it… Larissa didn't know herself well enough to be without her purpose. Maybe a trip would really help her gain some perspective about herself.

'I guess it would buy us some time to find a new clinic that'll take us both,' she conceded, and Ally clapped.

'I knew I could convince you. But we're not just there to work. It has to be an adventure,' Ally said again, and Larissa didn't like the conspiratorial glint in her friend's eyes.

'Isn't going to a new place an adventure enough?'

'No, because I know you, you will work non stop and not even take one day to explore your new surroundings. So I've come up with a dare— for old time's sake.' Ally was getting so animated, Larissa couldn't fight the smile spreading across her lips. When they'd met on Larissa's first day at the clinic, she'd had no interest in making any friends—until Ally had dared her she wouldn't join her at this exact coffee shop for a cup of coffee. With her competitive spirit ignited, Larissa had come to see Ally outside of work. And they had been friends ever since.

Ally remained her only friend, but that did not bother Larissa. She only needed one when she had already picked the best there was.

'I see, a dare. What do you dare me to do? Find a new best friend?' She crossed her arms in front of her chest, pushing her chin out in a playful challenge.

Ally rose to it, slapping her hand onto her chest in mock indignation. 'The audacity—don't you dare derail this conversation. For the new year, and in the spirit of embracing new things and getting rid of old stuff, I dare us both to have a no-strings-attached fling while we're away.'

CHAPTER ONE

Go to the Arctic Circle, they said. It'll be fun, they said. Larissa was *not* having fun. Somehow, 'fun' had missed the plane from Oslo to Svalbard. It had still been there when she'd boarded the plane in London, and she'd definitely seen it as the captain had announced that they would land in Oslo early enough for her to stretch her legs before she needed to board another flight.

But then she'd stepped out of the plane, wrapped in a thick jacket, an endlessly long scarf, and mittens Ally claimed she had made—even though Larissa could tell where the tag had been cut off—and ready to conquer the cold. But what she experienced right this moment wasn't cold. It didn't even live in the same postal code as cold. Whatever slammed into her the moment she exited the airport towards taxis and buses that would shuttle everyone to Longyearbyen was an evolution so far from anything she'd ever known, Larissa couldn't find the right words to fit. All she knew was that she was going to strangle her best friend the moment they were back in England two months from now. This had been her hare-brained idea, and she would let Ally know she would never listen to her again.

Why had Larissa picked that place again? Right, because the population was so low, chances were high she wouldn't have to cash in on that stupid dare she'd agreed on.

'Dr Costa?' Larissa perked up as her name rang through the night—or was it daytime? She flicked her wrist, but several layers of clothing covered her smartwatch. Without the sun ever rising, it would be hard to tell what time of day it currently was.

An older man stood a few paces away from the line of people waiting to get on the bus. He looked down at his phone, then back up at her, and waved. Leaving the line, she dragged her bag behind her and approached the man. He stuck out a gloved hand towards her and said, 'I'm Olav Fjell. My wife, daughter and I run the hotel that New Health Frontiers booked for you.'

Larissa took his hand in her own, giving it a squeeze she hoped could be felt through the thick mittens. 'Oh, nice to meet you. I was told one of my colleagues would pick me up,' she said, her eyes darting around.

'Yes, Erik Fjell? My son runs the hospital in Longyearbyen. He asked me to pick you up since an emergency came up at the clinic.' The bright smile turned into something else when he mentioned his son. Mischievous? Uh-oh. Was she about to learn that the hospital was actually just an igloo? Larissa's brain rotated through all of her worst case scenarios in a split second and decided that if the hospital was indeed an igloo, she would leave.

'Ah, I see. I appreciate you jumping in. Please call me Larissa,' she said, and didn't resist when Olav reached for her bags and led her towards his parked car. After she neatly tucked away her belongings in the boot, she circled around the car to the passenger side, only to bump into Olav.

'Oh…right. Other side,' she huffed out with a laugh, and when the old man smiled at her this time, the warmth in it put her at ease.

The interior of the car was marginally warmer than the outside. No doubt because of the lack of wind batting against her. She was at least accustomed to the icy wind from her town in Somerset. But there was cold and then there was…*this*.

Olav squeezed in behind the wheel, and warm air poured out of the vents when he turned the key in the ignition. Larissa had to suppress a shiver of delight at something as simple as heat. But the old man seemed to notice anyway, for he chuckled.

'Welcome to Svalbard, Larissa. I'm sure you've

read a lot about our little archipelago, but it's a whole different thing to experience it first hand,' he said as the car moved forward, taking the of-framp leading away from the airport building.

'It really is. I appreciate you picking me up. Makes me feel like a VIP,' she replied, and dared to peel the mittens off her hands. Then she stretched out her fingers in front of the air vent, soaking up the warmth.

'You definitely are a special guest for the Fjell family. We rarely have people staying for more than a week or two. That's enough for tourists to experience Svalbard as an attraction,' he replied, and then he said something else, but Larissa didn't catch any of his words.

A field of white opened up as the car lights illuminated the path in front of them. Lights twinkled in the distance, few and far between. Some cottages stood at the side of the road, their windows lit and smoke billowing out of their chimneys.

Winter never ceased in Svalbard. Larissa had read that the ice might melt on certain parts of the island, but this close to the North Pole, they didn't have what she would call a summer. Hands now warm, she rummaged through several layers of clothing to find the pocket containing her phone. It powered on just in time for her to snap a picture of another cottage further off the road.

She turned to Olav and asked, 'How do people live in these far away cottages?'

Olav considered, never taking his eyes off the road. 'The same way people live in other countries. It's not all that often that the harsh conditions of Svalbard impede anything. We have a cinema, restaurants, a library and some basic hospital facilities, as you probably already know. You can also eat your meals at the hotel.'

She'd checked out the hotel information along with everything else when New Health Frontiers had sent the information package over. The family-run hotel included meals and also had a social aspect to it where current residents could eat, drink or just meet up in a cosy common area. Outside of work, that would be the most likely space where Larissa could actually meet people.

Not that she wanted to meet anyone. Before she'd met Ally, Larissa had led a good life by only relying on herself and not getting sucked up into any drama. Her best friend had turned out to be so low-key that Larissa had believed maybe her self-imposed solitude wasn't necessary. Maybe she could be part of a community. Then her ex-girlfriend Rachel had happened, and she soon realised that Ally was an anomaly and not the rule.

They neared the town, with Olav prattling on about life on the island and easing some of her tension.

This was her new life. A change of pace to figure out what she wanted to do next in her professional life. Because her private life was quite clear—she wouldn't change a single thing. Ally and *The Great British Bake Off* were the only things she needed to satisfy her social needs. Paul Hollywood completed the trio between her and Ally, whether he knew that was irrelevant. Anyone with such a strong opinion about doughnuts would be her friend. Even if he didn't know they were friends.

'Why did you accept the placement here?' Olav asked, as if reading her mind.

Because my ex-girlfriend, who convinced me we would be together forever despite my reluctance, cheated on me in our shared flat while I was working late to fund our lives. Plus, perpetual darkness sounded exactly like my mood. Those thoughts flashed through her mind as she said, 'The GP clinic I worked at lost its funding, so I was unexpectedly out of a job.'

Olav raised his brow, convincing Larissa that he knew he had received the overly simplified and sanitised version of why she was here in Svalbard.

'That's a shame,' he said with genuine sympathy shining in his eyes.

Larissa nodded, looking down at her phone as they entered the town of Longyearbyen. The low hum of the engine and the muffled sound of snow crunching beneath the tires underpinned the silence between them. She stared at the empty bars at the top right corner of her phone and smiled when they finally filled with two lines.

Time to find out how Ally was fairing in India on her assignment.

Larissa: About to arrive at the hotel, and the cold is already too much. How is the heat of Kerala treating you?

Larissa: Also, jealous that it's hot and I hate you.

She waited for her friend to reply, but the three little dots indicating an incoming message didn't appear. So she slipped her phone back into her pocket just as Olav pulled up in front of a charming wooden building. Its exterior was adorned with twinkling fairy lights and looked like someone had copied the building right out of some Nordic-themed romantic movie.

'We're here. Welcome to the Aurora Hotel,' he announced with no small amount of pride in his voice. Larissa recognised the tone because she'd sounded almost exactly the same whenever she had spoken about her GP practice.

Now she and Ally would need to start over somewhere new and build back up—if they could even find a placement in the same practice again.

But that was a problem for future Larissa. Current Larissa was stuck on an ever-white island in the Arctic Circle, and desperately needed a shower after so many hours of travelling.

'See you tomorrow, Erik.' Ingrid, the hospital receptionist—and secretary, janitor and office manager—waved at Erik Fjell before trudging down the snow-covered sidewalk into town.

There was only one vehicle left in the car park of the hospital. His snowmobile. Snow crunched underneath his boots, a familiar sound that soothed his nerves as he unzipped the outer pocket of his heavy winter jacket to grab his keys.

Today had been uneventful, and a part of Erik suspected it was some cosmic joke. If he was being honest with himself, he would confess that almost every day at the Longyearbyen hospital was uneventful, and that's how everyone in the town liked it. With a population that never breached three thousand inhabitants, including researchers and tourists, there just wasn't much to do when it came to medical needs. But even though he usually handled the sniffles, different sprains, frostbite and the annual vaccine rounds, occasionally it could get more interesting than that. The population was small, but outside of the town, dangerous wildlife patrolled its territory, and accidents happened.

Today would have been a good day for that. Not because Erik wished bad things on anyone, but it would have distracted him from his new arrival—and what that meant for him. His GP on staff had left rather unexpectedly a few weeks ago, needing to go back to mainland Norway to take care of some personal matters. Though he understood things like that happened, the sudden departure had put him on the spot of finding a new GP on brief notice. Since the hospital ran on a skeleton crew only, there weren't any redundancies in his plan. If something was too big for his hospital, they would airlift the patient to Tromsø.

Erik had no choice but to look for a temporary placement with New Health Frontiers until he could get a permanent staff member. That temporary GP had arrived earlier today, and because the hospital was short-staffed, Erik didn't have the time to pick her up from the airport to welcome her to Svalbard. Instead, he'd had to ask his father to do that for him. Something he'd avoid under any normal circumstances if it hadn't been for the fact that his new temp GP was also staying at his family's hotel.

His mood darkened as he swung his leg over the seat of his snowmobile. He didn't know anything about the new doctor other than that she was a woman. Which was also enough for his parents to start meddling. There would no doubt be the same song and dance about pushing him toward violating his strict 'no dating outsiders' rule. Which was a subsection to his general 'no dating' rule. Being the only permanent doctor on the island, he didn't have much time to give, especially not to a relationship.

Sticking the key into the ignition, he checked the strap of the rifle slung across his back to ensure it was secured for the ride. Unlike most people, he stayed in a cottage outside the main village, which required him to be armed in case he happened upon a polar bear.

The streets of Longyearbyen were empty of any cars, but there were still plenty of people milling around town. Streetlights, placed a few metres apart, emitted a bright light, indicating that stores, restaurants, and cafés were still open. Most natives didn't need the reminder during their polar night season, but even though the sun wouldn't rise until February, some tourists still dared to come here in these dark months.

An older couple waved at him as he stopped at an intersection, and Erik raised his hand in greeting before zipping down the road. A ripple of tension rose inside him as the snowmobile ate the distance between him and his destination. Aurora Hotel had been in his family for generations, with the parents passing on the knowledge, the passion and eventually the entire operation to their children. Erik grew up in that hotel, spending many years helping with whatever tasks arose. Once school and homework had been done, he'd follow his father around to watch him do maintenance tasks or help with turndown service.

When he'd announced he wanted to attend medical school in Oslo, his parents hadn't been enthusiastic until they realised how much that path in life had meant to him. Then their concern had flipped over to him working too much and not spending enough time with them. Or not having a family of his own.

Gentle glowing fairy lights covered the wooden building, pulsing as they changed colour from light yellow to a deep turquoise, emulating the northern lights their hotel was named after. He had to admit, this was a nice touch. Probably his sister's doing. Anna was the one who was dragging the hotel into the current century as she took over more of the responsibilities.

Shaking off the snow already gathering on his arms, Erik hopped off the snowmobile and took a deep breath as he pushed through the doors of the Aurora Hotel. The warmth meeting him inside was a stark contrast to the sub zero temperature outside, and he tore the mittens from his hands. As he unzipped his jacket, a familiar voice said, 'Welcome to… Erik, dear.'

He hung his jacket on the coat rack, stuffing

his mittens in the corresponding sleeves before turning around to face the reception desk. He'd noticed the slightly eager tone as his mother, Hilde Fjell, stepped towards him and enveloped him in a hug.

'Your new colleague arrived earlier,' she said as she let go of him, and he pulled his lips up in what he hoped to be a convincing smile. The meddling was already starting.

'Thank Dad for picking her up,' he replied, then followed his mother as she led them deeper into the hotel. 'How is she?'

He knew next to nothing about Larissa Costa. Only that she came from England, that she had run her own GP practice there, and that she had been willing to move here as soon as possible. That had been enough information for Erik to agree to her placement. He'd been working double shifts ever since his GP left him. He didn't mind putting in extra hours, but the community of Longyearbyen deserved better than him running himself ragged—and potentially making mistakes.

'She came prepared, that's for sure. We watched her peel out of five layers. Every time we hung one piece of clothing, a new one appeared. Like an onion,' his mother said with a titter.

'I won't be long. Just want to welcome her and give her some information about tomorrow,' he said, hoping to get out of here in a few minutes. Then home to his cottage to eat whatever leftovers were in the fridge while cuddling up to his dog, Midnight.

'Your sister just informed her that dinner is almost ready. Why don't you join us, so we can all welcome her?' Hilde tilted her head towards the dining room.

'I don't think so, Mum. I'll just say hi to her and be on my way,' he replied, recognising the invitation for what it was: a way for his parents to, once again, push him towards some ill-conceived match because they thought everyone needed to be coupled up. Just like them.

'Are you sure? I think Larissa would really like it if you stayed. She's already asking so many questions.'

Erik was about to refuse again but paused when someone in the corner of his eye grabbed his attention.

At the base of the stairs stood a woman with rich, dark skin that seemed to glow under the warm light. Her cream-coloured sweater matched the rustic surroundings, giving her an aura as if she had always been here. A fact Erik knew to be false. He would have remembered the captivating iridescent light in those brown eyes. It drew him in like an open flame on one of the colder nights on the island.

Watching her required far more concentration than it should have, yet he didn't even care that all thoughts left his mind the moment her lips parted in an unsteady yet bright smile.

Something odd was happening in the dining room, and Larissa wasn't sure what it was. Olav's wife, Hilde, was hovering behind a man as she came down the stairs, her smile a similar brand of mischievous she'd seen on Olav earlier. What on earth was going on with this family?

It had something to do with the stranger, because as Larissa reached the bottom of the stairs, she saw Hilde's eyes meet her husband's, and they both grinned.

The newcomer, however… her eyes went to him. And stayed there.

Clear blue eyes framed by long lashes stared at her, rooting her to the spot. His features evoked an immediate response of familiarity inside her—along with something sharper, hotter that she instantly shoved away. Whatever that sensation was, it was Ally's fault. She'd been the one to dare them to find a fling during their placement. Seeing as her dating pool would be only a handful of people, Larissa doubted she would find anyone suitable.

Except this man stood in front of her, unmoving, his eyes dipping just below her chin before coming back up. He swallowed.

A flutter rippled through her chest, one Larissa ignored. Instead she spoke up as the silence between them stretched. Remembering that they were supposed to be colleagues for the next two months, she shook off her trance and stepped towards him with her hand outstretched.

'You're Dr Erik Fjell, yes?'

His name seemed to rouse the man. He blinked once, his eyes focusing, and for a second, he looked around in…confusion? Was he *not* Erik Fjell? Or did he simply not know where he was?

'Eh, yes… that's me. Dr Costa, I presume?'

The first thing Larissa noticed about him was his accent. Similar to the accents of the other natives she'd interacted with, yet his hit her in a completely different region of her body. A lot lower. Then he grasped her hand, and her focus shifted from his voice to where they touched. Rough calluses scratched over the inside of her palms, fingers lingering just for a second before squeezing her hand and shaking it.

A zap shot up her arm, as if he'd transferred static electricity to her, but she knew that wasn't what had happened.

'Larissa,' she said as she took her hand back, her fingers still tingling from his touch.

A smile appeared on his lips, rather unexpectedly, and Larissa didn't like what it did to her stomach. How it summoned a fluttering out of nowhere. White teeth peeked out from his lips, his mouth surrounded by the bristles of a close-cropped beard the same sandy colour as his short hair.

'Erik. A pleasure to meet you. I just wanted to stop by to welcome you after I couldn't fetch you from the airport.'

'We were about to sit down for dinner, Erik. Please join us,' Hilde piped up from behind Erik, and the sparkling smile on his lips faded. Then retreated into a thin line. The loss of it was instantaneous, with Larissa's own smile faltering.

'I'm afraid I can't stay,' he said with only a glance at his mother before those ice-blue eyes narrowed back on Larissa—making her stomach swoop again. 'Welcome to Svalbard. The hospital isn't far from here, only a ten-minute walk. But if you prefer to drive, I can pick you up in the morning.'

She didn't mind walking, and was actually looking forward to it. But that didn't stop the next words coming out. 'Thanks. I would love to ride with you.'

His brows rose ever so slightly. Had he not expected that? Larissa couldn't blame him. She didn't know why she had agreed, except that it maybe gave her a few moments alone with him before the everyday business of the hospital demanded all of her focus. Was that strange? Absolutely. Especially since she could hear Ally's voice whispering in her ear, telling her she could do with a quickie or a fling, and Larissa might well have found the only eligible bachelor on the island. Dang it. She'd picked this remote location so she *wouldn't* meet anyone.

Prompted by the thought, her eyes darted to his hand, and she bit her lip—both to stop a relieved smile from appearing and also just to remind her that this was *absolutely* not happening. She'd agreed with Ally to get her off her back and had zero intention of following through with their deal.

'I'll pick you up tomorrow, then. Six thirty sharp.' He smiled again, a much dimmer version than the one she'd seen before, and didn't even nod at his mother standing behind him before vanishing through the door—leaving nothing but a few stray snowflakes behind.

CHAPTER TWO

'I DON'T KNOW how to explain it. It's just…odd,' Larissa said as she looked out of the window and into the darkness. Well, not complete darkness. The street lights had come on at five in the morning at a low glow. Larissa knew that because Ally had called her, shaking her out of her sleep with her own personalised ringtone. Apparently, Ally had forgotten that they had a four-hour time difference now, and she couldn't just call Larissa whenever she felt like it.

But Larissa was desperate enough that she'd shaken off sleep to talk to her. She'd wrapped her blanket around her shoulders, had dragged the comfy armchair in front of the window and had watched the lamps lining the streets go brighter with each passing minute. The mechanism—and its purpose—caught her attention. It had to be some sort of simulated daylight to keep everyone in town on track with their circadian rhythm.

Now it was almost six, and Larissa was all

clued in on what had happened in India while she'd been en route to Svalbard.

'I mean, it gets pretty dark in winter in England, but I guess it's much more different when you see no sun,' Ally mused. On the video call, Larissa could see her friend pulling things out of her suitcase and stuffing them into a backpack. She'd told Larissa she was off to do a vaccine drive in a more remote location.

'It'll be an adjustment, but whatever.' A part of her still wasn't sure this had been a well-thought-out idea. No, that wasn't true. She *knew* she hadn't thought this out at all. The anger from her breakup compounded by the loss of her GP practice had driven her to make a rash decision. One that she now had to sit with for the next two months. In complete darkness. All on her own.

Well, except that there was Erik…

'Oh, don't sound so glum! Something about Svalbard spoke to you when we looked at the job postings. I'm sure you'll find that spark there. Just give it time. You've not even been to the hospital yet,' Ally said, and Larissa sighed. Ally had always been the more positive one in their friendship. The yin to her yang. There were times she really appreciated that. Today was not one of those days.

'I just… Okay, so. Erik Fjell, the person who runs the hospital. You remember him, right?'

Ally hummed before her eyes went wide. 'Oh yes, the Thor look alike.'

Larissa rolled her eyes. 'You're really comparing a Norwegian guy to Thor? Isn't that a bit cliché?'

Her friend waved a hand in front of her face. 'Whatever. What's he done already?'

'He couldn't pick me up from the airport because he was busy, so he sent his father. Turns out, they own the hotel I'm staying at. But he came by last night to welcome me—' Larissa pointedly ignored the 'aww' sound coming from her best friend '—and the vibes his parents were giving were off. They kept staring at him *and* at me with this weird energy.'

Whatever had happened in the dining room completely eluded Larissa. Probably because she didn't have parents in her life that could give off strange vibes.

Her own parents hardly factored into her life anymore at this point. While she was growing up, they'd been so busy with their own marital drama that they didn't devote as much time as they should have to raising her. They'd taught Larissa early on that she only had herself to rely on, and she guessed she owed them some gratitude for that.

A lesson she'd had to relearn with Rachel first crashing into and then out of her life in a spectacularly painful fashion when she'd found her ex-girlfriend interlocked with some other woman in their flat. Only for Rachel to blame it all on her. That if she hadn't worked so much or got used to leading such an independent life, she wouldn't have resorted to finding some closeness elsewhere.

Yeah, right.

'Oh really? So you waded into someone else's family drama. That's…healthy.'

'Oh, shut it,' Larissa grumbled, but she couldn't help the smile spreading over her lips. 'I'm not wading into anything. Just here to do my job.'

Ally raised her eyebrows high enough that they almost vanished in her hairline. 'And don't forget about our deal.'

'Yeah, about that…'

'Larry!' Ally shouted, glaring at her through the screen. Even with thousands of kilometres between them, she could feel her ire. 'You promised you would at least try.'

'The thing is… I didn't realise how small this place would be. Longyearbyen doesn't exactly have a thriving singles scene.' It was a harmless lie, though by the frown on Ally's face, she could tell her friend wasn't buying it.

The lights brightened again, and her eyes darted to the time on her phone. Erik would be here soon, and she wasn't even dressed yet.

With a groan, she pushed herself off the chair and walked to her own luggage. Pulling out a few things, she draped them over her body, surveying them with a critical eye.

'What about Thor? You thought he was cute,' Ally said, not willing to let this go.

'His name's Erik.' Larissa pulled out a pair of jeans she knew made her butt look exquisite and rifled through her pile of clothes for a top—settling on a pastel pink cable-knitted jumper.

She presented herself to Ally as she tamed her hair into a manageable bun on top of her head. 'What do you think?'

Her best friend furrowed her brow. 'What do I think? About…your clothes? I thought you were going to work.'

Larissa raised an eyebrow. 'I am.'

'Then why do you care if you look cute?'

'What? That's not…' She paused, examining herself in the mirror. Why *was* she concerned about how she looked? She wanted to leave a good impression, of course. But not with Erik. With her patients. With her new coworkers. Though Larissa had no intention of keeping any of these people in her life—the whole point of going away to work for two months was so she didn't actually have to hassle with befriending anyone—somehow this strange struggle with her wardrobe told a different story.

An amused glint entered Ally's eyes. 'What did you say is Thor's name? I need to google him.'

'And that's my cue to hang up before you can get any ideas. Love you, babes.' She picked up the phone, pressing her lips to the camera while making loud kissing noises. From the sounds coming from the phone's speakers, she knew Ally was doing the same thing. When she pulled back, she got a glimpse of her friend's smile before the call ended.

Why did she need anyone else in her life when she had Ally?

Fresh out of medical school, Larissa had accepted the first placement that would put a considerable distance between her and her parents, who still lived in the North East of England. It hadn't been anything personal, at least that was what Larissa had convinced herself of. Her parents were decent enough people. They were just terrible parents who thought having a child would save their marriage, but instead they just slipped further into their misery while sometimes forgetting they even had a child.

So Larissa had early on got used to cooking her own meals and doing her homework by herself, and just became comfortable with her own company.

But then she met Ally. With her welcoming

smile and her sunny disposition, she had wea-
seled her way into her life in what Larissa could
only describe as a war of attrition. Because in her
mind, she had come down there to work. She had
no interest in making friends or inviting people
in—romantically or otherwise. Connections like
that went against her highly self-contained life,
where she didn't have to mind anyone else's feelings around anything.

Until Ally had popped up, not giving up until
she had broken through Larissa's icy walls. So
Larissa had made an exception. She could have
one friend, but that was it.

Rachel had been another exception in her life
when she had met the woman at a Pride event
where Larissa had volunteered to oversee the
first aid tent. Letting Ally get close had lulled
her into the sense that maybe other people could
be okay, too. That maybe she didn't have to do
it all on her own.

But that hadn't worked out. At all. And now
Larissa knew better. The only person she needed
was a best friend and no one else.

A faint sound coming from outside grabbed
her attention, and she rushed over to the window,
peering outside. The faint hum of an engine cut
through the otherwise silent morning, and Larissa followed the vehicle with her eyes, watch-

ing as it grew larger and larger and eventually pulled into the hotel's parking lot.

'What the…' The streetlamp cast enough light onto the car park to make out the male figure, who just slung his leg over…a snowmobile? This couldn't be Erik, then, because he had offered her a ride to the hospital. That would only be possible in a car, right? Where would she even fit on a snowmobile? She scrutinised the narrow seat of the vehicle as the helmet-wearing figure stepped away. A second person could realistically sit there, if they were really close, like…her front flush against his back.

That thought triggered a spark at the base of her spine, shooting out and across her body in a star-shaped pattern.

Please don't be Erik, please don't be Erik. Gloved hands came down on either side of the helmet, one arm obscuring her view as he pulled it off. Sandy blond hair came into view first, and Larissa swallowed her groan as the rest of Erik's rugged face appeared.

Well, shit.

She should have walked.

Vice-like hands held on to Erik's jacket, pinning him into place on top of the snowmobile. He almost tripped trying to swing his leg over the seat, not expecting the resistance. Their helmets clanged against each other as he twisted, trying to catch her eye over his shoulder, but Larissa stubbornly held on to him as if her life depended on it.

The corners of his mouth twitched as he fought off the smile. Her discomfort was understandable, even if it was hard to grasp for him. He knew how to handle tourists—from both his time at the hotel and his work as a doctor. But Erik realised he never actually helped anyone get used to Svalbard. Not since Astrid, and even with her, he had failed. She hadn't wanted to stay here despite the promise to build a life together.

Sliding the visor of his helmet up, he said, 'You can let go now, Dr Costa.'

A muffled sound came from underneath the helmet he'd brought specifically for her.

'I can't hear you with the helmet on. You should let go and take it off.' Her fingers on him flexed, digging deeper into his covered ribs, and Erik pushed away the bubble of heat inflating in his chest. His body was reacting to unusual external stimuli, as he would expect. He could hardly remember the last time he gave someone a ride like this. It would have been with Astrid as well…

Erik stiffened as he caught the unwelcome thought, pushing it away. She was gone, had left him behind to seek her happiness elsewhere—

away from this island and its community that had sucked so much of the joy out of her life. Away from him.

The grip around him relaxed, and Erik took the opportunity to fully twist so that she completely lost her hold on him. More muffled words tried to escape into the open, and he reached out, pulling the helmet from her head.

A cascade of tight, dark brown curls tumbled into sight, their shine glossy even in the streetlamp's light. Her lips parted, steam forming in front of her with every exhale. Her eyes were wide and pinned on Erik. The unease of his memories vanished as they remained looking at each other. The condensation of her breath caught in her eyelashes, forming ice crystals that surrounded her eyes. The rich bronze of her skin stood in contrast with the white snowflakes, giving her the aura of an otherworldly beauty.

'Larissa,' she said, snapping him out of his trance—one he only noticed he was in because she'd said something.

'Pardon?'

'You said, "Dr Costa." But I would prefer it if you called me Larissa. Dr Costa is my father.'

Erik raised his eyebrows. 'Your father is a doctor, too?'

'Um… no.' Now those eyebrows came down, bunching together as he scrutinised her. 'It was a joke. Not a very good one, I have to admit. I talk too much when I'm nervous.'

That caught Erik's attention. 'What's got you nervous?' he asked, his head tilting to the side.

Larissa took a deep breath, and the space between them was narrow enough that he felt the warmth drifting across to him even in air that was −13°C. Her eyes widened slightly, then dipped to where he still held her helmet in his hands. As if she, too, realised that they hadn't moved away from each other for this entire conversation.

Even through all the layers, he could see her swallow from the way her jaw moved, and a part of him wanted to peel her scarf away to watch her throat work. Erik blinked at the randomness of that thought, but before he could shove anything away, Larissa said, 'I don't know if you noticed, but... the sun didn't rise today. It's freaking me out a bit because for thirty-three years, it's been right there with me when I get up.'

A smile spread over his lips before he could even think about stopping it. 'Did you forget to pack it?'

Larissa's lips twitched. 'I was sure I put it in my suitcase, but now I can't find it.'

'Ah, there is your mistake. Always pack the sun into your carry-on. If the people working at customs realise what this gigantic ball of gas in your luggage is, they might grow long fingers,' he said, leaning much further into the joke than he would have expected from himself. It was something about how her lips moved when she smiled. He wanted to observe it again.

But she didn't smile. Instead, her mouth rounded as a thin line appeared between her brows. 'Long fingers?'

'Does that idiom not exist in English? In Norwegian we say someone has *lange fingre* to say they're a thief. You know, longer fingers make it easier to steal things.' When the corners of her lips twitched again, a thrill went through him, and he added, 'Supposedly. My fingers are short and not at all thief-like.'

Erik stopped breathing when she threw her head back and laughed. The sound filtered through the cold air in all its clarity, winding its way through the many layers of his clothes and somehow skating across his skin—sending a shiver down his spine.

His own lips cracked into a grin, and he joined her laughter. He couldn't have stopped it even if he'd tried. Something about her laugh compelled him to join in, immerse himself in the sound and feel of it.

'By the end of my stay, if you teach me, I will become well-versed in mistranslated Norwegian idioms,' Larissa huffed out as her laughter subsided, and then she blinked. Some crystals coating her lashes fell off, melting against the warmth of her cheeks.

Her eyes darted down to where he still clung to the helmet, their bodies almost as near as they had been during their ride. As if the sudden proximity had only sparked alive between them in this moment, both she and Erik reared back a bit. He let her swing her legs over the seat and take a few steps in the snow before he got off the snowmobile himself.

'I gather this was your first time on one of these?' he asked, wanting to diffuse whatever strange moment they had shared.

Had he been flirting with her? He didn't even know this woman. Didn't *want* to know her. She would be here for two months before leaving Svalbard. The island, its community of inhabitants, the places—they would all become nothing more to her than a fun story to tell.

Where was this sudden intensity even coming from? The two metres Larissa had put between them didn't feel like enough anymore, so Erik took a few steps towards the hospital entrance, vaguely waving his hands for her to follow him.

'Yes, I've never been anywhere cold enough to warrant a snowmobile. One of the many new experiences I'm about to have,' she said, her voice a lot softer than when they were joking—like she, too, realised their conversation had taken a turn neither of them could explain.

'We can get you some lessons if you want to try it out yourself. Or we can get you a rental car, though some situations require a vehicle that can go off-road.' He pushed through the doors of the hospital, and a pleasant warmth enveloped him almost immediately.

Erik waved at the receptionist and waited for Larissa to step up to the desk. 'Ingrid, this is Dr Costa, the new GP that'll be with us for the next two months.'

The woman stood and extended her hand towards Larissa, and he watched with mounting amusement as the doctor struggled to peel off her thick gloves. As the seconds went on, his self-restraint grew thinner—to the point where he wrapped his fingers around her wrist and pulled the right glove off for her.

Electricity passed from her to him through the tiny sliver of skin he'd touched on her wrist, but it was enough to shoot up his arm, his fingers tingling where they had made contact.

Larissa's eyes widened as they locked into his, and she mumbled a thank you before turning to Ingrid and finally shaking the woman's hand.

CHAPTER THREE

AFTER THE STRANGE conversation when they'd arrived at the hospital and the even stranger moment involving his hand around her wrist, Larissa's day had calmed down significantly. So much so that she now wished there was a bit more *something* happening. As long as that *something* didn't involve Erik.

The phantom of his touch still lingered on that small patch of skin on her wrist, and she fought off the memory whenever things got too quiet.

'How can I help you today?' she asked, looking at the patient in front of her. An older gentleman with thin grey hair covering his head. He'd limped into her office not even ten seconds ago.

'Something's wrong with my toe on this side,' the patient, Martin according to the schedule Ingrid had given her, said, slapping his right thigh. 'It's been tender for a few weeks, but now I can barely get a shoe on to walk the dog in the morning.'

Like Erik's, Martin's words had an accent to

them—one that identified all the local people. There were enough people at the hotel's dinner to suggest a decent number of visitors as well, though she had yet to meet anyone. Her dare with Ally floated around in her head and with it, memories of the snowmobile ride. How they had stood there staring at each other with only a hand span between their bodies.

Her worst trait—making strange jokes when nervous—had come out, but instead of backing off, Erik had leaned in. Had even joked with her. Larissa was sure that if she had peeled away the layers of clothing from her body, she would have been kept warm from the heat inside her.

'That's not good. Why don't you slip out of the shoe and let me have a look?' Larissa focused on Martin in front of her. They had booked her a full day of appointments for today, though the cases weren't necessarily what she'd expected. So far, she'd seen three sprained ankles, two swollen knees and five routine check-ups. The patients were nice, but there wasn't a lot of variety.

So when Larissa got a glimpse of Martin's red and swollen toe, something inside her jumped and pushed away the thoughts of Erik—of her dare with Ally—that she'd been batting away all morning.

'Could you lie down here so I can have a closer look?' She patted the exam bed beside her, then turned around and slipped into some gloves as the patient moved behind her.

Dragging the backless rolling chair closer to the bed, she looked over the foot. The cause of Martin's discomfort was staring right back at her. Skin was growing over his toe in unusual places, his flesh red where the nail extended into it. With a glance at the patient, she took the foot in her hand and turned it around, testing the ankle mobility before placing it back down.

'Seems like you got an ingrown nail there, Martin,' she said when she was confident that there was nothing else going on. 'But no worries. We can remove that right here.'

'Oh really? I won't have to make the trip to Tromsø?' His eyes widened, forehead bunching up.

'No, I can take care of such small things. No need to take you away from home longer than necessary.' Something in his voice gave her pause, and she looked at the toe again, playing back his words. Did he not like leaving Svalbard? She'd assumed everyone took trips to Norway on the regular, even if it was just for a change of scenery.

'Let me get everything necessary. The way it looks, we will only have to remove a part of the nail and then pack it. Do you have anyone who can walk your dog for a bit while you recover?

You should really keep off your feet.' Larissa frowned when Martin shook his head. 'We'll find a solution for that, too,' she said as she got up and began rifling through the drawers to find an anaesthetic, forceps and a scalpel to get to work.

With the last patient out of the door, Larissa devoted the last hour of her shift to updating all the patient notes and getting to know tomorrow's list of patients. By the looks of the notes Ingrid had left on the appointments, she was looking forward to another day of general check-ups, flu-related symptoms and some random body aches. If this was what every day looked like, her time here in Svalbard would be easy enough.

Her gaze wandered from the screen to her phone, and she picked it up to text Ally.

Larissa: I had to ride on the back of Erik's snowmobile today. I think I left bruises on his ribs.

Ally: Oh dang.

Ally: Does he have nice ribs, though?

Larissa blinked at her phone as the last message popped up, her lips drawing down in a frown.

Larissa: Nice ribs? What on earth are you on about? They're ribs.

Ally: Just reminding you that nice ribs could be adventurous ;-)

Putting her phone down, Larissa rolled her eyes as the topic from this morning came back up. The dare she'd agreed to loomed over her, mingling with the moment she'd shared with Erik earlier. No part of their conversation had been suggestive, and yet somehow joking with him had sparked something inside her. A heat that had been chasing her all day.

Was she really considering Erik for her fling? She'd said no in her call with Ally, and she'd meant it then. He worked with her, and she lived in his parents' hotel. Talk about awkward when it came down to doing the deed. But her main reservation had been that he'd seemed the opposite of interested in her—or anyone. Erik had been polite but distant yesterday. Aloof.

But this morning, some of that frost had melted, giving her a glimpse of what she suspected was so much more than he let her see on the surface. Beneath the icy sheets, there flowed a lively river.

Larissa's eyes wandered towards the door, considering. He was still somewhere in the hospital. She doubted he'd have left without checking in on her, though where the confidence of that knowledge came from, she didn't know. He seemed to be in charge of the hospital. *Seemed*, because she wasn't actually sure. New Health Frontiers certainly made it seem like he was the one in charge. But Erik hadn't really shared any details about the hospital. He'd just sat her down in her GP clinic, showed her the computer system for the patient charts and told her their facilities were limited to regular GP stuff. Anything that required surgical intervention needed to be transported via helicopter to Tromsø.

With all her charts done and no more patients to see, Larissa clicked around the computer system while debating whether she should see what Erik was up to. Why was she even hesitating to seek him out? This had nothing to do with her dare. She just wanted to go talk to her colleague—one she would spend a lot of time with for the next two months. Which probably meant she shouldn't think about him in any way other than professionally. Then again…it was *only* two months. That was an ideal time frame for a no-strings affair with a willing participant.

Letting out a huff, Larissa pushed to her feet and grabbed her phone before leaving the office.

Larissa: You got in my head with that Erik thing, you witch.

Larissa: I'm going to see him now to… I don't know. But whatever the outcome, I'm blaming you.

Not waiting for a reply, she stuffed her phone in her pocket and went to search for Erik.

The hospital consisted of three different sections. The two smaller ones were general practitioner clinics with waiting areas for their patients. Larissa hadn't seen whether the other clinic had been open as well or if it served as a space to put in walk-in patients without an appointment. With how light her schedule had been today, she couldn't imagine having a second GP here.

The front desk was empty already. Ingrid had shown her around the hospital's staff area when Erik had been called away, and Larissa already appreciated the woman's sunny demeanour. She left the impression of being an important pillar of the community, knowing every single patient by name whenever Larissa had escorted them out.

The main building appeared as deserted as the front desk, with the only light coming from beneath the door that led to Erik's office. As far as she could tell, he was both leading the hospital and acting as the emergency physician during the daytime.

Finding the door slightly ajar, Larissa knocked and then pushed it open.

Erik sat behind his desk, sandy-blond hair tousled as if he'd spent most of the day running his fingers through it. It was probably soft. Those short strands would slide like silk through her fingers. Would it be an enticing contrast to the neatly trimmed beard covering his face, leaving her own skin rough and sensitised in just the right way?

Wait, what?

Larissa cleared her throat, willing the lewd thoughts into the back of her mind, and that was when Erik looked up—and the full force of his icy blue stare hit her. The intensity in his eyes was enough to wipe any trace of order from her brain. All she could focus on was his gaze on hers and how her heart beat against her chest as if it was trying to stage a breakout.

She pressed her hand to her chest as if to say *you stay right there*.

The corner of his lips twitched, as though he'd thought to smile but had then decided against it. 'Dr—Larissa. Please, have a seat. I was going to find you after finishing up here,' he said, pointing at the chair sitting across from his desk. With her brain still rebooting itself, she obeyed and used the time it took to seat herself to remember where she was—at her job. In front of the person who was *technically* her boss, even if it didn't feel that way.

The faux leather covering the backrest of the chair squeaked as she leaned back, crossing one leg over the other to project a sense of ease she didn't quite feel on the inside.

'Patient charts?' she asked, unable to identify the papers lying on his desk.

'Sort of. This hospital is part of the Norwegian healthcare system, so we have to submit papers about procedures at regular intervals,' he replied, tapping the pen on the stack of papers in a rhythmic beat. 'It's the most boring part of running this hospital.'

'I would offer to help you, but there are at least three letters on that page that I don't recognise.' Larissa knew the woes of government paperwork all too well. She'd spent many nights sitting on her couch, getting through it so it didn't eat into her time with the patients. On the really bad days, she and Ally had made a game out of it, rewarding each other with pieces of candy whenever they finished a report.

The corner of his lips twitched again, and she wondered if that was just his version of a smile. Or was he fighting off the smile?

'I will survive.' He glanced down again, the tapping of his pen the only noise as the silence settled between them. Larissa wasn't sure what had even brought her here. She didn't need a ride home. The hotel was down the road from the hospital. As was everything else in this town, really.

'How was your first day running the GP service? Anything you need?' he asked, and Larissa was glad he'd broken the silence. For some reason, she didn't want them to stop talking—but she could equally not come up with anything to say. Her brain was still in the process of starting up again, too distracted from how the hair and the beard and those deep, clear eyes seemed to trip something inside her.

'It was good. Uneventful...which I think is the desired state of a GP clinic, especially if more complex cases mean they have to be shipped all the way to Norway. That's a long way to travel for a broken toe. I once broke my toe, and my GP just told me to be careful without actually doing anything about it.' Because her brain was preoccupied, her mouth developed a will of its own, forming word after word without her involvement or her explicit consent.

Erik's mouth twitched for a third time in this conversation. It was then that Larissa realised maybe staring at his mouth kept tripping up her brain.

'They are actually transported via helicopter to the hospital in Tromsø. Not by ship,' he said.

She blinked at him. Was he saying nonsensical things to poke fun at her rambling? 'Oh... Yes, I know that. Ingrid explained it to me.'

A huff of air left his nose in a rush and...was that a chuckle? Whatever the sound was, it found its mark inside her body, sending a spray of glowing sparks down her spine. 'You said *shipped*, and

I thought it prudent to make sure you don't think they are actually using a ship for transportation. That would be highly inefficient.'

The rate of her blinks increased until she could actually see her eyelids half of the time. Her mouth opened, searching for the right words to respond, but the echo of that huffed laugh still vibrated over her skin, as if trying to find a way inside her. Then it dawned on her. 'You're messing with me, aren't you?'

The reward for her keen observational skills was a laugh. A real one. Not a twitch of his lips or an exhale that could be interpreted as a chuckle. No, she got a full-throated laugh, deep and melodic, and it fuelled this ridiculous idea that had popped up this morning. That she wouldn't mind having a casual fling to make good on her dare if it was with Erik.

'My apologies. People say I have a rather…dry sense of humour,' he said, his laughter fading into a smile that did funny things to her stomach. 'I forget that it sometimes doesn't translate well.'

Larissa needed to get out of here. Because clearly Erik understood the devastating effects his smile had on people, and that was why he forced himself to keep it hidden. Even with the considerable amount of space between them—a whole desk—the surrounding air heated. Damn Ally and her dumb fling dare. It was all her fault, putting the idea of some closeness in Larissa's mind. Without it, she wouldn't have perceived Erik as anything except her coworker. But now...

She shoved her hand into the pocket of her lab coat, looking for her phone, when her fingers brushed over a piece of paper. Fishing it out, she stared at the address scribbled on it. 'Oh, right. There is something you can help me with. Can you show me where this address is? I punched it into my maps app, but it didn't land anywhere,' she said, holding the piece of paper out to him.

Erik took the paper, and a frown pulled at his lips as he scanned it. 'This is a cottage outside of Longyearbyen. Isn't that where Martin lives?'

Of course he knew whose address that was. 'Yes, that's right. I performed a nail avulsion on him and had to pack his toe because the area had got infected. He says he lives alone and can't walk his dog, so I offered to come by before work to help with that.'

Erik shook his head, strands of hair falling onto his brow. 'You're not allowed to wander outside of the town limits without a rifle,' he said, and nodded towards a corner of his office where a rifle leaned against the wall, just behind the door.

'A rifle? But why...' Her voice trailed off as parts of the instructional pamphlet she'd read on the plane came back to her.

'There is a saying here that we are just guests

on Svalbard and must be mindful of the true inhabitants of the archipelago—polar bears,' Erik said, reminding her of quite the most important part of the information package.

Damn. That would not cut it. Martin was counting on her to walk his dog. If he put pressure on his toe, he might cause the infection to spread. If it hit his bloodstream, there were all manner of bad outcomes… Larissa eyed the gun again, then swallowed the lump in her throat as she asked, 'How can I get a rifle?'

Was this woman serious right now? 'What do you mean?'

Larissa tore her eyes from the rifle and levelled that dark brown gaze on him. He rolled his jaw as her eyes swept over him, assessing him as if she could see through his skin and into him. Which was, of course, a ridiculous overreaction. A random adrenaline spike was putting his body in a focused mode that picked up every little detail about her. From the texture of her hair right down to the dark lines crisscrossing through her irises, he had somehow memorised everything in the few minutes they'd been speaking to each other.

And had more than once wondered what her jawline would feel like if he slid his fingers over it. Or better yet—his mouth.

Erik batted the thought away. This wasn't just

highly inappropriate. I t was actually stupid. This was his place of work. His responsibility to his community was the most important thing in his life. There was no space for any ideas of attraction. Not when he knew first hand how much of his focus those feelings demanded. Though his family served the community in their own way, his dedication to looking after his people had caused a rift between them that had never truly closed. The same dedication had ended his engagement to Astrid. When she'd put him in front of the choice of picking her or Svalbard, the choice had been simple. Hard but simple in the end.

'I mean, how do I get a rifle? Don't you think I should have one if I'm here to treat people?' She paused, looking at the weapon again and rearing back from it. 'What if I need to attend to a patient in one of the cottages?'

'You won't. If anything like this comes up, I will handle it.' He could almost see the discomfort around Larissa, her lips pressed into a tight line and her spine stiff. Erik had to give her credit, though—she was putting thoughts of their patients ahead of herself. With one last glance at the paperwork, he stood and rounded the table. He leaned his hip against it, glancing down to where Larissa was sitting at the edge of the chair. 'You already promised Martin you would do it?'

She sighed, her eyes dropping down to her feet. 'Yes, he's expecting me there tomorrow morning before work. I didn't know how else to keep him off his feet. When he said he lives by himself and needs to let his dog out, I knew he wouldn't take the bed rest order seriously unless he had someone to take care of his dog.'

Erik had no power over the smile that spread across his lips—not for the first time during their conversation. The quiet enjoyment he got from her presence was throwing him for a loop. He couldn't even explain how she did it when they had just met yesterday. The last woman who had sparked an interest in him, his ex-fiancée Astrid, had taken far longer to break through his shell. They'd met when she came into the hospital with frostbite, and even though they got along right away, he didn't understand she was interested in him *this* way until Anna pointed it out.

Not that Larissa was interested in him. And he *definitely* wasn't interested in anyone. His time and energy now all went into work—the one thing in life that he could do his very best for. His dedication had only redoubled when Astrid left him, complaining that she would always be second to his job. But what had she expected? Svalbard was his home and the people…they were his.

At least he knew Larissa understood that side of him. Promising Martin that she would stop by to walk his dog before work told him everything he needed to know about her dedication—and that he wanted to learn what she was like as a person.

Erik knew he should offer to walk the dog. He was already familiar with Martin's husky, Storm, as they often met when he was outside with Midnight. He would walk her anyway, so taking an additional dog along would be no big deal. That would be the most practical solution, leaving Larissa out of it, and yet he still said, 'How about we do it together? I'll pick you up in the morning before work, and we can do a round with his dog. If I accompany you with my rifle, that's enough to satisfy the law.'

Her head whipped up, tight curls flying around her, and her eyes widened. Her lips fell open in an O shape, and Erik's thoughts screeched to a halt when his eyes dipped to her mouth. Fantasies of that mouth came over him unbidden, and he swallowed the lump popping up in his throat.

'You would do that for me? Erik, that's—' She jumped to her feet before finishing her sentence, grasping one of his hands with both of hers and giving it a squeeze. 'Thank you so much.'

A smile spread across her face, slow and bright, as if she was here to replace the sun for the months that he hadn't seen it. The sight was intoxicating, the heat he'd banished to the pit of his stomach exploding through his body as her palm pressed against his. That small touch provoked all sorts of misguided thoughts in him, all of them involving both of their hands on various other parts of each other.

Erik opened his mouth, willing the words to push past his throat, but the spark of joy in her eyes robbed him of the breath required to say things. Which was good, because he wasn't sure if the *right* things would come out. He just had to keep himself in check until she let go of his hand. Any second now.

Except the seconds ticked along, and her hands remained wrapped around his. Her grip slackened somewhat, almost teasingly so, but she kept herself firmly planted in his space, looking up at him. His eyes dipped lower as she swallowed, the sound of it vibrating through the space between them.

Finally she said, 'I took this posting with New Health Frontiers because of my friend.'

Erik had no idea why she had said that, but he also didn't care. Because apparently he just liked it when she spoke. How words sounded when they left her full lips. It was the reason they'd stayed outside in the cold, talking about sunshine.

'Oh yeah? How come?'

She swallowed again, her gaze obscured by her dark lashes as she lowered her eyes. 'We worked together at a clinic. When we got the news that it had lost its funding and would need to close, Ally urged us both to be adventurous before we find another placement together.'

'I'm sorry to hear that,' he said, trying to stay grounded in the conversation when her soft palm was still lying against his.

Larissa swallowed again, his eyes tracking her throat. It was alarming how much he enjoyed that. 'I, um…'

Her voice trailed off as she lifted her gaze to look at him once more. What he saw in there sent a spear of heat through his chest, setting his nerve endings abuzz until he could feel the sparkling in his fingertips.

Erik couldn't help himself. Not when her scent drifted up his nose—vanilla and something intangible that was uniquely her. Not when his fingertips grazed over the back of her hand and he felt the shudder trickling through her deep in his bones. He leaned in, closing the already narrow gap even as his good sense was desperately trying to reach him.

The lights above their heads flickered, then went out completely—plunging them into darkness.

Larissa gasped. Then her hand released his, and he heard the sound of metal scraping over the linoleum floor as she no doubt collided with the chair behind her. Losing sight was like a bucket of ice water poured straight into his veins, clearing his head and saving him from the colossal mistake he had been about to make. A mistake because of a desire, and he wasn't even sure where the desire had come from.

Was he so touch-starved that he would feel such an intense need for a woman he had only met yesterday? It was so unlike him, Erik didn't recognise himself in that situation.

'This happens from time to time. Stay still so you don't hurt yourself.' Navigating the office by memory alone, Erik sat back down behind his desk, opening the drawer and taking out the heavy-duty torch inside.

Cool light illuminated his office as he flicked it on. Larissa stood at the door, and from her widened eyes, he could tell she had just played back the entire situation in her head and was as horrified as he was.

'What do you do when you're in the middle of a procedure?' she asked, her voice straining with an emotion he couldn't quite pinpoint.

'There are torches on the wall and in drawers everywhere. But we also have a backup generator.' He picked up his phone, looking at the time. 'I'll check on the generator, and then I can drop you off at the hotel.' Erik wasn't sure if having Larissa pressed against him even for the short ride to the hotel was a good idea, but he couldn't make her walk just because he was losing control of his senses.

She fished her phone out of her pocket, tapping on the screen for a few seconds, and then the bright light on the back of the phone turned on. 'No, it's okay. I…think I want to walk. But I'll see you tomorrow.'

She didn't give him a chance to say anything else, rushing out of his office and around the corner until he could only see the dim glow of her phone's torch. Erik slumped against his chair, burying his face in his hands.

What the hell had just happened between them?

CHAPTER FOUR

ALLY DIDN'T CALL her this morning, which was a shame because she would have found Larissa awake and ready to leave the hotel. Only she didn't want to leave the hotel, or even her room. She wanted to crawl straight back underneath the blanket and just will herself to England. If she closed her eyes and wished for it hard enough, it would happen. Right?

It hadn't happened, and now Larissa sat in a comfortable chair in the hotel lobby, watching the small flame in the fireplace dance around. She definitely *didn't* imagine what it would be like to be curled up naked in front of the fire with a certain Nordic god look alike, their skin sliding against each other's as she learned every peak and valley of his body.

Nope. This train of thought could absolutely not leave the station. Or could it? It was the back-and-forth that had robbed her of her sleep—when her mind wasn't replaying the moment in his office on loop.

Erik had leaned in, hadn't he? There was no way she'd made that up. Maybe she had?

No one would call her a relationship expert. Her parents' rocky marriage had taught her exactly one thing: that romantic love wasn't worth the trouble. A much younger Larissa had believed that doomed her to a lonesome life.

Until she'd discovered casual sex. Oddly enough with a woman she'd met in a mostly deserted library during her first year in med school. Men had quickly entered the mix—being more readily available than lesbian or bi women—so being attracted to both sexes had actually worked out rather well for her.

Until Rachel.

The chemistry between them had been instant when they met, and even though Larissa was familiar with sexual attraction, there was something deeper there. Something more elusive that she wanted to explore because it had been such a novel concept to her.

Her curiosity got the better of her. As she hung out with Rachel, she learned more about the woman, and each piece of knowledge only intrigued her more. Enough that she said yes when Rachel proposed something Larissa had never considered: dating.

Despite not liking people in her space, she had tried to make it fit—make *Rachel* fit into her life.

But it hadn't been enough. Rachel had wanted more of her, more of her time, more of her life. And Larissa had been stupid enough to give all she had. Right up until the moment she learned Rachel had cheated on her.

At least the breakup had left her with another lesson. One that reinforced the experience of growing up self-sufficient. Larissa couldn't rely on anyone outside herself. Except for Ally. But she was an exception, not the norm.

Erik brought back that sense of curiosity and intrigue inside her, and that was a red flag fluttering right in front of her eyes. She should have been neither curious nor intrigued by the guy who was basically her boss. Even if that was in no way how she was perceiving their dynamic. With five staff members total, there wasn't really the space for a big boss ego.

The chime of the door floated through the otherwise quiet lobby, and Larissa tore her gaze away from the flickering fire just in time to watch Erik enter. His eyes fixed on her with an intensity that had her tensing up.

'Oh, Erik,' a female voice said, and they broke their eye contact, both looking over to the counter, where a young woman stood. Her long hair was tied into a braid down her back, and her eyes were the same blue Larissa had got lost in yesterday.

Erik approached the counter, and he and the woman exchanged a few words in Norwegian. Despite not knowing a single word of the language, Larissa tried to listen to their conversation anyway, wanting to get familiar with the sound of it. The woman—Larissa thought from the familiarity she must be the other Fjell child Olav had mentioned on the way here—sounded chipper, her voice dropping deep at times as she filled most of the conversation. Larissa realised she hadn't been here yesterday, so she hadn't officially met her.

Something about Erik's voice when he spoke Norwegian did funny things to her stomach.

She closed her eyes to focus on the conversation, Erik's low and lilting voice soon washing over her like she was listening to a podcast he had recorded just for her. The lack of sleep throughout the night caught up with her, weariness settling deep into her bones, and his voice… she could listen to it for the rest of her life and never tire of it.

A log cracked in the fireplace, and Larissa sank back into the chair, soaking in the warmth. Her limbs grew heavy, her thoughts drifting away as she kept listening, trying to hang on to the words she couldn't understand.

'Are you ready to go?' The words had transformed into something she could understand, the voice now closer to her. She just had to—

Larissa's eyes flew open, and she recoiled when two piercing blue eyes stared right at her—through her skin and into her soul. She blinked several times, trying to shake the disorientation spreading through her. She'd been sitting in a chair in the lobby waiting for Erik, and then...

'Coffee still kicking in?' Erik asked, and she blinked again, shaking her head.

'I haven't had coffee yet,' she said, prompting Erik to shake his head, too. The side of his mouth kicked up in a half smile that she didn't dare to inspect any closer. Not when his voice had just lulled her to sleep. He could never know that.

He turned to the woman again, saying something before turning back to Larissa. 'We'll bring some coffee on the walk with us.'

'Like in paper cups? Will the coffee even survive outside?' Her phone told her that the temperature today was –20°C. Her takeaway coffee turned lukewarm within two seconds of stepping out of the shop back in Frome, so there was no chance she could take a coffee with her unless she wanted a *very* iced coffee.

Erik huffed out a breath in a subdued laugh, and the memory of what his full laugh had done to her insides came rushing back at her.

'No, unless you want a coffee-flavoured popsicle instead. Though I'm not sure what that would do to the caffeine,' he said with the usual tug at the corners of his lips.

'I mean, have you tried it? It could be the revelation everyone in Longyearbyen has been waiting for.'

The fine lines around his eyes crinkled, becoming more pronounced and adding a breathtaking quality to his already handsome face.

Damn it, was she seriously considering coming on to him? That was a dumb idea for so many reasons. The main one was that they worked together, and if he rejected her, that would make the next two months awkward as hell. Or maybe he was into her, but they weren't sexually compatible—that had happened on enough of Larissa's one-night stands that she knew it was a thing—and they still needed to see each other every day.

Then there was the entire thing about her being way too curious about him and how those feelings were definitely not good for a no-strings-attached arrangement.

'In case it wasn't clear, the coffee comes with us in an insulation flask,' Erik said, bringing her back into the room. She blinked twice as he held up two travel mugs. Her contemplations had mentally dragged her far enough away that she had missed a few seconds of their interaction. She looked around just to catch a glimpse of Anna as she walked through the door to the back of the hotel.

'You ready to go?' he asked, reminding her of why she was even up at the crack of dawn.

Right. They had a dog to walk. That was why he was standing in front of her, pretending like nothing had happened yesterday. Well...nothing *had* happened yesterday, but a very loaded nothing, one that was pregnant with possibilities. If one more second had passed, that nothing could have transformed into *something*.

Larissa nodded, getting to her feet and following Erik outside. He stuffed the two travel mugs into one of the bags hanging from the side of the snowmobile, fastening the top of it, and then they were off—gliding through the snow in a direction she had yet to explore.

The area outside of Longyearbyen was similar to what Larissa had seen on her way from the airport. It was mostly snow and ice, but occasionally a little cottage stuck out from the snow, lights in the window illuminated and showing the residents inside starting their day. This far outside of town, there were no lights besides the ones lining the streets, and most of the cottages were visible only by the light coming from the houses themselves.

They passed three more before Erik swerved

left, going off-road and up a small hill. The head-lights of the snowmobile illuminated the great white expanse unfolding in front of them, and Larissa gasped when they came to a halt next to yet another small cottage. Fairy lights hung on the outside walls, giving off a warm and welcoming glow to anyone approaching. The big windows framing the door on each side, however, were dark.

'Do you think Martin is not awake yet?' Larissa asked as she approached the cottage, snow crunching beneath her feet.

'No, he is. I saw the lights on in his house,' Erik said while fiddling with something on the snowmobile. She turned to see him shoulder a messenger bag and slip their two travel mugs inside. He held an object in his other hand, and when he stepped closer, she identified it as a key ring.

'But this…' She glanced at the house behind her and then back at Erik.

He huffed—why was this sound always doing weird things to her insides?—and came to stand next to her in front of the door. 'This is my place.'

The icy cold surrounding her somehow gave way to a sizzling heat. Larissa stared at him wide-eyed as he stuck the keys into the lock and opened the door. 'Wait… Your place? Why are we…'

Her voice trailed off as he pushed the door open. A small light trickled from the opening—enough to illuminate the floor but too weak to penetrate the blinds that Larissa could now see were drawn over the windows. A pitter-patter sound of clawed feet against a wooden floor drifted outside just as a gust of warm air hit her face.

The head of a white-grey husky appeared in the door, looking up at Erik. Then its eyes shifted to her and it cocked its head, a strangely inquisitive spark in its eyes.

'You have a dog, too?' Larissa whirled around, looking at Erik. He bent down, locking what she now realised was a long leash into the husky's collar and tugged it outside, closing the door behind its tail.

'This is Midnight. She and Storm are actually friends,' he said, rubbing the dog between the ears.

'How—Oh my God, Martin has convinced *you* to take care of his dog as well, hasn't he? And yet you made me think I was all soft and squishy for the plight of an old man.' She remembered the glint in his eyes when she'd confessed that she'd promised Martin to walk his dog. She'd thought it to be disapproval. Turned out there was a good chunk of amusement mixed into it.

'I can neither confirm nor deny,' he said, the

corners of his eyes narrowing enough to hint at the smile behind the neck guard he had pulled over his mouth. Even with all the layers, puffs of condensation floated between them as the harsh weather froze every exhale.

Larissa crossed her arms in front of her. 'You can't tell me if you've ever looked after Martin's dog?'

'Doctor–patient confidentiality,' he said, his tone so serious she had to blink several times.

'I'm his doctor, too. You can't hide behind confidentiality.'

'Yes, but this happened before you joined.'

'Before I jo—Erik, I read his patient file. There is no retroactive confidentiality.'

Erik looked down at his dog, and Larissa caught him making a quick gesture with his finger. Midnight got onto her feet and bounded through the snow, the long leash unfurling from his hand as she moved. He turned to Larissa, shrugging his shoulders, but the humour sparkling in those blue eyes was apparent.

And Larissa couldn't help herself as she laughed, falling into a brisk step next to him as they walked towards a far away cottage that she could make out by the lights in the windows.

The cold conditions of Svalbard had never bothered Erik—not until today. Because as he walked down towards Martin's cottage with Larissa next to him, he really wanted to see her face. *Why* exactly he wanted to see it was beyond him, but if he had to name the need bubbling up in his chest, that would be it. This doctor from England had proved to be far more intriguing than he had expected. All he'd wanted from New Health Frontiers was a competent doctor to take some of the workload until he could decide on whether there was enough capacity to hire a permanent GP.

He hadn't imagined that he'd find himself on a walk with her, wanting to know what lay underneath the surface.

'Can I ask you something?' he said, even though he knew he shouldn't get to know her better. Whatever that thing between them had been last night was already too much.

It was the phantom brush of her fingers against his wrist that prompted him to ask. Maybe he couldn't get her out of his head because she was an unknown person in *his* space. He prided himself on knowing his community—in serving the people of Svalbard to the best of his abilities. They were *his* people. Of course he would want to know someone living among his community. Attributing anything more to it would be foolish.

Larissa shot him a sidelong glance, her dark lashes casting a shadow across her cheekbones. They both wore headlamps to illuminate the path ahead. Conveniently, it also prevented Erik from looking directly at her for fear of blinding her.

'You just did,' she said, and her huffed laugh sent clouds of condensation adrift between them. 'But I'm feeling generous, so you can ask me something else.'

His own chuckle appeared in white puffs in front of him, and he stared ahead to where Midnight bounded through the snow. 'What did you escape by coming here?' he asked, letting the question out without filter.

He knew her placement was temporary. From experience he knew people didn't come to Svalbard because they wanted to. They were always running from something.

Astrid had run from her boring life, wanting the change and thrill the archipelago offered. She had swept him up in her life, ripping him off his feet—and his world off-centre—before he could even understand what had happened. He'd wanted to believe that the slow life wouldn't bother her long-term. That she would see the value of the community they had here in Longyearbyen and appreciate it for what it was.

But then she'd left, telling him her life was bigger than this island. That she couldn't cope with his long hours or the calls in the middle of the night when they needed him for an emergency. But what had she expected? Sometimes he was the only physician on this island. The lives of his community—his people—sat on his shoulders. He hadn't turned away from that to satisfy his family's plans for him. He hadn't done it for her, either. Hadn't even wanted to try.

A low hum interrupted the steady crunching of snow underneath their feet. Larissa tilted her head upwards, causing the path in front of her to be plunged into darkness. 'And here I thought I could avoid any existential questions for a few more days,' she said, though Erik couldn't detect any apprehension in her voice.

The snow lit up again as she moved her head, and the quiet of the early morning snow settled in between them for several breaths. Then she continued, 'As I told you yesterday, my clinic back in England got shut down. When the trust funding the clinic reviewed their spending, they decided to close some of the GP services and re-direct them to other practices. My friend Ally is a nurse, and together we worked hard to bring out the best of our clinic. So having it shut down so unceremoniously was harsh to see.'

Erik looked at her from the corner of his eye. The need to study her facial expressions bubbled up in him. Why hadn't he initiated this conversation in a place where he could actually see her?

'That's a tough spot to be in. But there's a critical shortage of GPs where you are from, is there not? Why come here when you could have found a place closer to home?' Though he couldn't see much of her, some sense told him that wasn't the full story.

'How do you know England lacks GPs?'

He shrugged. 'Recruiters sometimes call me with job offerings. They are disproportionately UK-based, so I figured there definitely wasn't a lack of jobs.'

'I see…' Her voice trailed off, the silence once again reclaiming the space between them. Only Midnight's occasional pants broke through as she ran back, regarding Larissa with a modicum of curiosity, before leaping away and into the snow.

She was considering leaving it at that—a boundary Erik would respect, no matter how desperately he wanted to know more about her. But eventually, the light from her headlamp flickered across the snow as she shook her head with a sigh. 'Did you ever have your heart broken hard enough that you just needed to disappear into a different life?'

The snow under his feet crunched louder than usual as he almost lost his footing at the question—at how close to a target it hit inside his chest. He forced his gaze to remain on the path ahead. The answer to that question was way more personal than he'd planned on getting with Larissa. But it also revealed an even more intriguing side of her. Because the only reason she would ask was that she had experienced the same thing.

Was there any danger in letting her know? She was here for two months. There was no way she would become someone of great importance to him. If the demise of his engagement to Astrid had taught him anything, it was that he was incapable of forming such attachments. Too much of him belonged to the people on Svalbard, and no one would ever be happy with just a small sliver of him. They tended to want it all. Erik wasn't free to give all. A slice was all he had.

But a slice was enough for…other things.

'I have experienced that, yes,' he said, letting the truth come out for the first time in the icy landscape of his home.

He saw the deep breath she released more than he heard it. 'And where did you escape to?'

Erik lifted his hands, indicating their surroundings. 'Out here, where it is quiet.'

Larissa seemed to consider that, tilting her head to the side so she could shoot him a glance without blinding him. 'Well, I came here.'

'What happened?' The question was faster than his critical thinking skills, floating in the space between them like an overbearing sales person at a shop a customer had just entered.

'Well…' She sighed again, more condensation gathering around her. 'I didn't have an easy childhood and kind of just learned how to deal with life on my own. It's what's worked best for me, so I never saw a reason to change that until my... ex appeared in my life. It took us far too long to understand that we wanted different things from life, and we could have avoided a lot of hurt feelings if we had just worked through some of our stuff. Instead of being an adult, though, she decided the right way to resolve this was to bring some other person into our home and then blame me for the lack of attention I had paid her.'

Clouds billowed from her mouth again, though this time they came from a huff of laughter with a sharp edge to it. 'Jesus, why am I even telling you this? That's way too much to know about a coworker.'

This was definitely oversharing. With anyone else, that was what he would have called it. Yet somehow, with Larissa, it landed differently. It spoke to the desire within him to know her better. Though where that desire came from, he couldn't tell. She wasn't part of his community, so why did he care?

Midnight tugged on the lead, growing more excited as they drew closer to Martin's cottage. She knew she was about to see her friend Storm. With the exterior lights of the house illuminating their path, Erik flicked his light off so he could steal a glance at Larissa. Her eyes remained ahead, showing him only half of her face, but it was enough for him to see the thoughts tumbling around in her head. Had she never shared these thoughts with anyone else, and they had been sitting in her chest for so long that at the first opportunity, they'd come bursting out?

Her ex-partner was a woman? He hadn't misread the signs between them, had he? No. Making up something like that wasn't something he ever did. The taut tension, the stolen glances, and even this strange closeness swooping in with her confession were real.

Which was a problem. Because if his parents picked up even a whiff of the attraction between them, he wouldn't hear the end of it. After Astrid had left, they'd been relentless about finding him 'another shot at love.' Something as small as Larissa leaving by the end of February wouldn't deter them. But he knew asking someone to stay on the island wasn't an option. They needed to *want* to be here, not stay here for *him*.

'You risk nothing by telling me,' he said, hoping it would inspire her to keep on talking. 'I'm some guy you met on an island very far away from your actual home. What's the harm in letting some things out?'

They stopped in front of the cottage, and when Larissa reached up to turn off her light, she faced him. Her neck guard obscured half of her face, so all he had to go by were her eyes. The dark brown colour of her irises shone in the dim light while shadows brushed over her cheeks with each bat of her lashes. Her gaze was piercing, and even though he couldn't figure out the underlying emotion, the need to fidget itched in his fingers. Was she weighing his words? Trying to figure out if he was as harmless as he claimed he was? He'd meant what he said. If letting go of some things was what she needed, she'd come to the right place. Erik had never felt judged by the ice and snow.

'Are you saying you live in a little house outside of Longyearbyen because you're avoiding your ex?' she finally asked, eyes narrowing on him.

He let out a breath. She seemed to regret the glimpse of vulnerability she had granted him and wanted to make it even between them. Erik pressed his lips together, considering. If he was serious about him not being a risk to her, then she shouldn't be a risk to him, either. He should feel safe around her. If he let her see that tiny slice of him, maybe she would share one, too. To what end, Erik wasn't sure. A curiosity unlike anything he'd experienced compelled him—

all wrapped up nicely in the safe knowledge that Larissa was only temporary.

'No, I lived there before I met her. Living outside the town was more to gain a bit of distance from my family,' he said, focusing on those eyes to gauge her reaction. Bracing because he knew what question she would ask next. He had asked the same thing moments ago.

What happened?

But to his surprise, she didn't ask. Instead, she tilted her head to the side, her eyes sweeping up and down his entire frame. When they settled back on his face, she said, 'So that means you're not seeing anyone?'

His thoughts came to an abrupt halt. 'Seeing anyone?' The words came out as a question even though he hadn't meant to say anything out loud—the surprise had his lips moving before he could consider.

'Yes, like…*uninvolved.*' Larissa stressed the last word.

A shadow flitted across the illuminated window to their side, and they both turned their heads to see Martin's backlit silhouette waving at them. As one, they raised their hands and waved back.

'I, um, no. I'm not involved. There is no one.' He paused when the corners of her eyes creased. Was she smiling?

The door to the cottage opened, and Larissa climbed the three steps that led to the deck where the house was built. On the last step, she looked back at him over her shoulder. 'Good,' she said, amusement mingling with something else— something sharper—in her eyes before she turned back to Martin to greet him and Storm.

CHAPTER FIVE

'THERE IS NO way strawberries actually cost that much. What are they made of—solid gold?' Larissa stood inside Longyearbyen's only supermarket with her phone to her ear, staring at the fruit selection with a growing lump in her throat. People shuffled past her, some stopping and nodding at her in greeting before grabbing overpriced produce without even blinking and putting it in their baskets before moving on.

She shouldn't have been surprised. As a new face, she stuck out from the usual crowd. But two weeks in and not only did people already know her by name, she also knew some of them. Some she recognised from the clinic, while she'd seen others at the coffee shop she liked to visit when she was feeling particularly homesick.

'At least you have strawberries. I've been living off of oatmeal, lentil stew and prayers for the last two weeks,' Ally replied with an edge to her voice. Sounded like the ongoing work in Kerala required a lot of travelling from her friend.

Fragments of conversation hummed around her, some in English, others in Norwegian, and she could only imagine that they, too, were wondering how much they would have to tighten their belts to afford some strawberries. The store had printed new price tags for the strawberries, with hearts replacing the zeroes and the letters 'Valentinsdag Spesial' stuck next to it on a separate sign. Oh God, Valentine's Day was still a month away and they were already promoting it?

Today was Larissa's first day off since starting at the hospital—and she had no idea what to do with herself. After scrolling through TikTok for a solid hour while lying in bed, she could feel the brain rot setting in and realised she needed to move her body. It was an excellent tactic to avoid brain rot and also *other* thoughts she was trying to ignore.

Thoughts around Erik and the sound of his voice as he said, 'There is no one.' Heat stained her cheeks as she recalled that moment. The word *good* had formed on her lips as she embraced the dare she had made with Ally. One fling—for fun. Just because she let herself crave and indulge in some tender moments between the sheets didn't mean anything about her had to change. Larissa was done with dating, done trying to fit someone into her life who didn't *want* to fit. It took little imagination to see that anything more than a casual fling with Erik would cause a repeat of the disaster that had been her relationship with Rachel.

Good.

It *was* good. Except for the fact that they hadn't spoken about it since. He'd unpacked the travel mugs as they left Martin's cottage behind, and then Erik had spoken about the people living in this area just outside of town. He'd known every single inhabitant by name, telling her who to expect in the clinic and who was due for a checkup.

Had he changed the topic because he regretted the direction it had gone in? They rarely interacted at work, and half of the time when she went looking for him, Ingrid informed her he was attending to someone at their home.

'Okay, theoretically,' Larissa said to Ally, stressing the last word. '*If* I was interested in *maybe* banging a dude. No one specific, mind you.'

Ally gasped on the other side. 'You're going for Thor? Yas, queen!'

'No, I'm not. Stop even thinking about that.' Larissa wasn't sure why she was still pretending like it wasn't Erik when she was talking with Ally. Something about all of this remaining hypothetical just calmed her down. Like she could opt out at any time.

To her relief, Ally seemed okay to play along.

'I think the best way to go about it is to just tell this man of mystery. Did you already bat your eyelashes at him and touch his arm whenever you laugh?'

Images of their morning dog walks together fluttered through her mind. The distance between them as they marched through the snow had definitely diminished. So maybe not touching, but there were glances. The conversations had been pleasant. Fun, even. He'd introduced her to people as they returned to town, pointing out important and well-loved members of the community. Larissa had also learned more about the history of the hospital and how Erik spent most of his time there.

Through the conversations, one thing had become clear to her: Erik valued his community. And by how many people already had taken the time to get to know her, she could understand why.

'Okay, let me pose a scenario to you. You're hanging out with some cute guy, who shall remain unnamed, and then he tells you about—'

'Fancy meeting you here.' Larissa lurched backwards at the sound of the familiar voice—which turned out to be a mistake. Because that put her firmly within Erik's personal space. He had apparently been somewhere behind her. His broad chest collided with her back, the contact enough to give her an idea of what lay beneath the layers of clothes. Thor indeed, she thought as a shudder raked through her.

'Ally, I'll call you back,' Larissa whisper-hissed. She lowered the phone from her ear while smashing the disconnect button. How much of the call had he heard?

Larissa winced at the thought that it might have been every single word. Time to do some damage control. They might have been vaguely flirty with each other at times, but she wasn't ready to move her hypotheticals into reality.

'Ally is having man trouble. She doesn't know how to talk to him about it. You know how it is,' she said.

Erik cocked his head. 'Not really.'

'You're telling me you are *not* an expert in propositioning men?' she asked, the familiarity between them far too comfortable after two weeks.

His eyebrow quirked up, and the beard hair surrounding his mouth twitched in one of his subdued smiles. 'Nope. Never been with one,' he said, and why did those words send another wave of heat through her? What he had or hadn't done with *anyone* was none of her business, yet the casual openness of his experience did something to her limbs—as if she had misplaced all of her bones.

'Damn, neither have I,' she said, and laughed when his other eyebrow joined the first one near his lush hairline. He really did have perfect hair that she knew would feel like heaven between her fingers.

'You…' His voice trailed off, and Larissa burst into laughter.

'I'm kidding, okay? Though that look on your face…' She paused, her words trailing off when she thought of what she'd wanted to say. His expression had been one of shock for a reason. Was it because of disappointment? What did he have to be disappointed about? That she lacked experience? That implied he wanted something from her. Something more than just a casual acquaintance. Maybe a fling…

She knew how to agree to be passionate for one night. And she might not know how to do relationships, but the knowledge that this kind of human connection wasn't for her was comforting.

But a fling lay somewhere between a one-night stand and a relationship. A space unfamiliar to her.

Was his appearance here a sign that she should let her hypothetical thoughts become more real? Why did that thought send a thrill racing down her spine?

'That was amusing for you, yes?' His expression was deadpan, only making her laugh more.

Maybe she was overthinking this and just needed to go with the flow. If he was interested, he would get it. Larissa was going to leave in a month and a half, and that alone should have signalled her only interest was in something temporary.

With her teeth sinking into her lower lip, Larissa took a breath and said, 'Maybe we can figure it out together? If we puzzle it out, I might be able to give Ally some better advice.'

There was a not-so-clear message woven through her words, but by the widening and then narrowing of his eyes, she knew he'd picked up on it. Even through the noise around them, she heard Erik's exhale, felt it on her skin.

His eyes scanned around them, as if checking if anyone was watching, and then he stepped closer—putting himself squarely in her space. Their eyes locked, and the intensity in his ice-blue gaze was enough to make her breath stutter. Then he let his eyes wander down over her face to her neck, pausing as if to watch the rise and fall of her chest. But then his gaze dipped even lower, fixing on a point Larissa couldn't follow with her own eyes.

'What did you come here for?' he said, his unmovable frame and the scents of fresh laundry and snow the only things she could focus on.

'What? To…work?' Larissa wasn't sure why

he was bringing it up, but by the playful eye roll, she knew he hadn't meant that.

'To the store.'

'Oh…' Now she looked down at her hand, too, inspecting the still empty shopping basket. 'I wanted some strawberries and something else for dinner. I was planning on sitting in my room and calling Ally back.'

Erik's feet remained planted firmly on the floor, but somehow he still got closer to her just by slightly leaning forward. 'Do you think Ally would be okay if I commandeer some of your time today? I'll take you to dinner, and we can workshop this particular question you have. Maybe even come up with some answers before you report back to her. Since you're so kind to help your friend.'

Larissa blinked, her throat suddenly dry. She coughed, willing the heat rising in her to slow. Thinking straight was a lot harder with Erik crowding up her space, yet she had no plans of telling him to back off.

Quite the opposite.

'Y-yeah, I think she will understand. It's her question, after all.' Understatement of the year. The moment she told her best friend that she was giving in to the lure that was Erik Fjell, Ally would punch her fists in the air like she had just won the Nobel Prize in medicine.

A smile spread across his lips. It was only the second or third time Larissa had got a glimpse of his teeth as he smiled, his amusement usually not showing more than a twitch of his beard around his mouth. She was glad for it, because the full effect of his smile wasn't anything she was prepared for in this moment. It shot through her body like a tiny, fiery meteor, colliding with everything it met and leaving smaller fragments in its wake in distant corners of her body.

Her knees wobbled, and she gripped the handle of the shopping basket tighter to stop herself from reaching out. Would his chest feel as solid as she imagined underneath her palm?

'Good.' He reached out instead, and Larissa's breath stuttered out of her when his fingers grazed her arm. But he didn't touch her. Instead, he grabbed something behind her. When his hand came back into view, he was holding a box of strawberries. 'Now we're ready to go.'

The pub buzzed with the low hum of conversation when Erik led her through the doors. Some eyes turned towards them as they walked in, and many people greeted him with smiles or a pat on the shoulder when they passed.

An unfamiliar warmth pricked the top of her scalp, trickling down through her body in a steady drip. Because when she glanced up at

Erik, he was smiling back at the people, whispering a few words here and there before moving on. The smile was a more subdued version of the one she'd seen in the store, more familial and less...whatever it was brewing between them. The beginnings of this hare-brained idea of a fling? Larissa wasn't certain.

But from the brief seconds it took for them to cross the pub and find a small booth at the far end, she could tell that Erik was a pillar in his community. Everyone greeted him with a spark of kindness in their eyes, enough to send a pang of longing through her. She and Ally had joked that they couldn't go for a coffee or a night out in town without bumping into a patient. But she realised that she actually enjoyed those interactions, as brief as they were. Somehow, seeing that she was making a difference in people's lives— enough that they would recognise her outside the clinic—was gratifying in a way few things in her life were.

They stopped at the bar, ordering their drinks, and Larissa listened to the slew of Norwegian the person standing next to Erik directed at him when he recognised him. Erik kept on nodding, glancing her way now and then with an apologetic tilt of his head that she would have to let him know was completely unnecessary. Larissa could do with a break from these intense blue eyes trying to capture her soul. That was not on the table with them. Not that anything else *was* on the table. Not yet. Though she hoped this invitation was going the way she hoped it was...

Grabbing their drinks, Erik walked to a free booth, setting both glasses down as they slid in on opposite ends. 'Wow, you weren't kidding when you said you know everyone,' she said.

He huffed out a laugh, his voice vibrating through the space between them in a gentle hum. 'When the town you live in doesn't have more than three thousand inhabitants, you tend to get to know the people. Especially if you are the only doctor most of the time.'

Larissa nodded. 'Frome is much larger than Longyearbyen, but our clinic was in a smaller neighbourhood with a similar vibe to here.'

Erik took a drink from his beer. Larissa watched as the condensation from the glass clung to his fingers, slipping down in a random path across the grooves of his skin. '"Our clinic" being yours and Ally's?'

Larissa blinked at the question, not expecting it. 'Yeah...did I say "our"? That almost makes us sound like a couple.'

He shrugged as he looked at her over the rim of his glass. 'It's nice to have someone on your side, especially when you're running a medical service for a small community. That way you can observe trends and sometimes even forecast a particular illness going through the town.'

'The people here have been very welcoming to me, especially during the communal dinners at the hotel,' she said.

'It helps the long-term residents of the hotel to make some friends. Though those are rare. Anna hasn't mentioned anyone else staying there for longer.' Larissa had seen him interact with his sister each morning when they left. Just from their back-and-forth, it seemed she was teasing him about something, but Larissa hadn't had the courage to bring it up. His parents had acted similarly on the first night here, so there was *some* joke going on.

'Did you used to work at the hotel with the rest of your family?' she asked, hoping the question sounded innocent enough. She didn't want to run head first into a hornets' nest if there might be tension. That was more Ally's style of getting to know someone, or at least it was, before her boyfriend's death took that away from her. After that, she'd become more withdrawn and cautious about making new connections to the point where Larissa had seriously considered staging an intervention.

But even though she had spent two weeks with this man now and seriously considered giving in to the building attraction by just straight-up hitting on him, she knew little about him. Which should have been good, because knowing things about a partner was for people who wanted more than just sex.

There was the tiniest change to his expression, one she would have missed if she hadn't already been absolutely enthralled by his face. Just imagining tracing the lines of his jaw with her fingers—or lips—sent sparks flying through her.

'When I was younger, I used to help, yes. The Fjell family has looked after the Aurora for many generations. But after spending a summer volunteering at the hospital, I realised I wanted to do something else with my life. Serve my community,' he said, his voice dipping low enough for Larissa to feel it on her skin.

'And your parents didn't want that?' she asked.

'"Didn't want" is a strong way of putting it. They had expected something different from me, but they understood my passion. But now they are quite belligerent about my personal life since I "left the fold". Comments about how I don't visit enough or why I'm living by myself in the wilderness.' He paused, taking a drink from his bottle. 'They mean well, but I choose to live the way I do for a reason. It gets exhausting to keep on defending my choices. So I just stopped going by the hotel as much.'

Erik chuckled, his eye leaving the bottle and

narrowing on her. 'You kind of forced my hand by moving in there.'

Heat flared in her cheeks, and Larissa swallowed the lump appearing in her throat. He chose isolation just like she had after Rachel. That hadn't been what she'd come to find out about Erik. No, her intention had been to continue the conversation they'd started at the grocery store, keeping things on the hot side of sexy. Somehow, they had landed in the warm region of closeness, sharing things about themselves—just like they had when they'd walked Martin's dog.

She shouldn't dig into this anymore. Knowing things about Erik was unnecessary for the deal she'd made—wasn't necessary to satisfy the pinch travelling from behind her belly-button further down her body whenever she saw him.

Yet she opened her mouth anyway, giving back a piece of herself after he had given one to her. It was only fair, wasn't it?

'My parents messed me up pretty bad. Since I remember, they've struggled with their marriage and relied on me to look after myself.'

The cold of the glass bit against Erik's palm, and he released his grip on it, forcing himself to relax. Easier said than done. He hadn't been more on edge since the moment Larissa Costa had walked into his life—had it really only been two

weeks? Though they mainly worked on opposite sides of the building, they'd spent some time
together early in the mornings as they walked
Storm and Midnight. After their first morning,
all of their conversation had remained superficial.
She hadn't granted him another glance beneath
the surface, and neither had he. Had thought that
maybe this was for the best. The last thing Erik
needed in his life was an entanglement with the
potential to get messy. He'd been there, done that,
got the heartbreak that came free with it.

His life wasn't about that anymore.

But now she sat here, letting him peel off a
layer and look at her with a fragile vulnerability
that stole the breath from his lungs. A direct result of him oversharing just a few moments earlier. Was that what his words had signalled to
her? That they had something inside themselves
that made them the same outside of medicine?
Erik hadn't even intended to share anything, but
something in her eyes compelled him to seek
closeness with her, even if he could only achieve
it by being more personal.

'So, my parents are too involved in shaping
my life, and yours were hardly there?' he asked.

Larissa's eyes drifted away from him—something he noticed with a pang in his chest—and
scanned the gathered crowd in the pub. He didn't
come out often, preferred to spend his time in the

clinic in case someone needed him, but he'd lie if he said he didn't enjoy seeing everyone. It was the faces of these people that reminded him how crucial his role in Longyearbyen was. How he was unique in the way he could give back to all the people who had raised him alongside his parents. Give back to Martin, who had taught him how to handle a rifle. To Ingrid, who brought food to the cottage whenever he was sick and his parents couldn't look after him because of their guests. Or all the others who had so uniquely touched his life, tying him to this place on a molecular level.

'Maybe if they had met during our early years, they could have balanced each other out,' Larissa said, and her gaze darting back to him sent a thrill through his body. His fingers tightened around the glass again as he sought the cooling effect against the heat rising in him.

This conversation wasn't anything that should have him even near the state he was in. Her presence alone was enough to turn his head around, and Erik wasn't even sure where any of this was coming from. After the relationship with Astrid had collapsed in the fashion it had, Erik hadn't let himself think about any female attention, no matter how hard his parents tried to convince him. There wasn't much to begin with in Longyearbyen anyway, but he also couldn't afford the distraction. Didn't want to invite someone into his community—into his heart—only to learn that it would never be enough. Focusing on the people who needed him—the people of Svalbard—was easier than facing rejection again for something that was so intrinsic to his spirit, he didn't know if he could ever stop. Didn't want to think about it because he would not stop.

'So you learned how to look after yourself? Is that why you need to gather evidence before you can give your friend proper advice on her love life?' He purposefully brought the conversation back to what had got them talking to each other at the grocery store. The phone call he'd overheard had sent a buzz of electricity coursing through his veins, hoping that the guy mentioned was him despite Larissa's insistence that it was about her friend. He shouldn't want her attention in such a way. But the longer he spent time with her, the louder the voice got in his head, whispering one thing over and over again.

What's the harm?

Larissa was leaving by the end of February, and his life would go on as if she had never been there—except he might have found some closeness with someone who wasn't looking for more, either.

His words had the desired effect on Larissa. Her eyes flared wide, her hand around her glass slackening. Her cheeks flushed, the rich, dark colour deepening until it glowed from within. When her tongue darted out from between her lips to lick her lower lip, Erik swallowed the groan building in his throat. 'I'm not looking for anything serious. I tried that once. It didn't work,' she said when she found her words again.

'What a strange coincidence, because neither am I,' he said, fighting off the smirk tugging at his lips. Though he wanted to know more about her, wanted to dive deeper into who Larissa was behind the quick wit and stunning exterior, this was the type of conversation he felt more at ease in. These were the grounds on which he wanted to explore the attraction linking them—not the overly personal basis they were heading toward.

To his surprise, Larissa chuckled, head drooping down as she inspected the contents of her glass. 'What I'm trying to say is that I'm out of practice. After the breakup, I haven't really put myself out there. Not even in a casual way,' she said, her eyes only briefly darting up to him before she lowered them again.

That piece of information had him raising his eyebrow. 'Is that the ex you mentioned earlier in the week?' He could still remember her words, the rawness when she'd asked about his broken heart. They had found common ground in a place he hadn't meant to share—even though he'd been the one to ask that question.

For him, Larissa was somehow both push and pull, bringing him into her orbit no matter how ill-advised he knew it would be.

She nodded, something delicate in her eyes shuttering. Whatever had happened between them, she had no intention of speaking about it. What brief glimpse she had offered him was all there would be. Fair enough. Erik didn't plan on retreading old ground with her, either. It wasn't necessary for the thing he sensed swirling between them.

'You know so much about my heartbreak, and I haven't asked you anything about yours,' she said, taking the last sip of her beer before setting the glass down with a thunk.

Erik gave her a one-sided shrug. 'I don't think either of us is all that interested in knowing the other person's deepest wounds,' he replied, going out on a limb with that. A quiet part of him actually was interested, but he needed to convince himself that he wasn't interested in Larissa beyond anything physical.

She laughed again, shaking her head. 'I didn't flee here to confront my very complicated feelings. That sounds far too sane and stable for my taste.'

'So you're telling me you are neither sane nor stable?' Erik leaned forward, bracing his arms on the table between them. He noticed with a considerable amount of satisfaction that her eyes darted down briefly, taking in his forearms before her gaze came back up—and her throat worked in a swallow that sent a zap of electricity down his spine.

'Do you think sane and stable people come to Svalbard for a two-month placement in the middle of polar night?' she asked, and drew a chuckle from his lips.

'That was actually something Ingrid was concerned about when we spoke to New Health Frontiers. That there wouldn't be many people willing to spend two months of their lives in complete darkness.' Though the concept was easy to grasp in theory, it was a completely different thing to actually live through it.

'Well, there you go. I was basically your target demographic for this job posting.' A grin spread over her face, as if she was particularly pleased with having wrestled this concession from him.

'I'm glad it was you who took it.' He said the words without putting any thought into it and held his breath when a strange quiet spread between them. Ugh, that was the wrong thing to say to someone he wanted to be casual about. 'What I mean to say is—' he began to explain when a shout interrupted him.

Erik's name tore through the air with a sense of urgency that had Larissa on high alert. She joined him when he jumped to his feet and pushed his way through the crowd. Behind the bar, a middle-aged woman wearing a white chef's uniform waved her hand, pointing at something Larissa couldn't see on the floor.

The jovial chatter around them died when Erik knelt down behind the bar. Larissa rounded it a moment later, seeing the bartender on the floor clutching her hand to her chest. Blood already soaked her apron, staining the light grey fabric dark.

Her eyes darted around, taking in the details behind the counter. Shards of glittering glass covered the floor, with two large pieces standing out. One had bright red blood covering it while the other lay scattered in the doorway to the kitchen—where the chef hovered, worry lining her face.

Erik said something in Norwegian and then shushed the woman in a soothing tone as he peeled the hand away from her chest. The hint of an expression fluttered over his face before a calmness descended on him—one she was all too familiar with. It was the physician mask people in her care received. If patients got even a hint of what they were thinking as doctors, it would lead to panic that quickly spread all around them. They couldn't afford any of that, no matter how bad the injury might be.

'Can we stitch it up here?' Larissa asked, crouching down next to Erik. Now she could see the blood still seeping out of the wound, soaking the towel he pressed against her hand.

'The cut is deep. It would be better to move her to the hospital. I can't apply a lot of pressure to the wound without something to numb the pain,' he said to her. His eyes met hers for a few seconds. Then he looked over at a patron standing at the bar. 'Lars, call the ambulance to pick us up. We can give her a local anaesthetic and some pain relief while we head to the hospital.'

Larissa couldn't help her grateful smile as he kept all the conversation in English, with the villagers around them not seeming to mind. While Lars got on the phone, someone else began ushering the throng of people away from the door, so they had a clear path to transport the patient once the ambulance arrived.

Which, to Larissa's surprise, was in less than three minutes. Even in a small town like Frome, the system could get overloaded quickly, with the ambulance services needing to triage patients and send help where it was most pressingly needed. That was the upside of working in a small village where everyone knew each other's name. The medical emergencies were infrequent, and the system balanced itself well enough.

A nurse Larissa had seen at the hospital, Melanie, jogged into the pub while pushing a stretcher in front of her, and she went down on her knees next to the bartender. She said something to Erik, who nodded and then looked at Larissa. 'Mel and I will move her onto the stretcher. Can you keep pressure on Daniela's hand while we move her? Make sure you don't grab too tight,' he said, and Larissa nodded.

Grabbing disposable latex gloves from the first aid kit already opened and spread out on the floor, she unwrapped the gauze from its packaging and nodded at Erik when she was ready. Just as Larissa pressed the gauze to the wound, he pulled the towel away so she was now applying pressure to the wound. When she had wrapped the gauze around the hand a few times, she signalled for them to lift Daniela onto the stretcher. They then packed her into the ambulance and headed towards the hospital.

CHAPTER SIX

IN THE END, Daniela needed quite a few stitches to close the wound on her hand. Erik had ordered her to sleep off all the meds they had given her before he'd let her out of the hospital, and even though he'd told Larissa that he had a grip on things if she wanted to leave, something inside her had compelled her to stay.

She didn't want to contemplate any further that this *something* had the shape of an almost two-metre–tall Nordic god, but no matter how hard she tried, Erik kept popping back into her thoughts. Their conversation at the pub had veered into territory Larissa hadn't realised she could even talk about. Not just about Rachel and that she had existed, but also her parents. How she had grown up learning to be self-sufficient because they were too wrapped up in their own drama to look after their child. She'd told him how that behaviour had shaped her and had influenced her relationship. Had led to heartbreak…

The most surprising thing Larissa had learned

was that he, too, seemed to be running away. He was also hiding something of himself with thick walls that warned everyone not to come near him. She'd seen them after their first morning out with the dogs. He'd let her glimpse something on that first day, but all the subsequent days, that glimmer of what lay beyond the wall had disappeared, the barrier reinforced.

Which was fine. Totally fine. Larissa didn't *want* to know him like that. Sure, there was something unbelievably intriguing about him. She couldn't stop herself from picking away at the loose stones she encountered every so often— hoping there would be another gap for her to peer through.

Like when she'd seen him smile at everyone in the pub, so at ease with who he was around his community. Larissa had lost that feeling when they had closed the clinic down, with nothing but Ally left to tether her to Frome, to her life there. She'd felt comfortable enough to contemplate roots, to let Rachel in and see if they could somehow figure things out.

What a waste of time that had been. Rachel had wanted a completely different person from what Larissa could ever be, and it hadn't mattered how hard she'd tried, how much she had explained what *she* needed. It had never been enough.

It was easier not to try. Like right now, as she vowed not to get to know Erik better. She didn't need to know anything for their fling to become a reality.

Yet there was still this need bubbling right underneath her skin, demanding she peel away at him.

'You're still here?' As if her thoughts had summoned him, Erik appeared through the door of the office.

Her eyes glided over his body as he took off the lab coat, tossing it in a bin in the office's corner before turning back to look at her. A low thrum of energy went through her as the ice-blue gaze snagged on hers. There was some wariness in his eyes, maybe a result of the emergency that had cut short their…whatever that had been at the pub. Date? Meeting between colleagues? Those didn't sound right. Not when she thought about how close he'd been to her in the grocery store. How his breath had brushed over her flushed cheeks when he'd leaned in to invite her. The subtext of that interaction was more than clear—he was interested in something physical.

Larissa gave a casual shrug—or at least she hoped it looked casual—and said, 'It's not like I have anywhere else to be. My room is not that exciting, and I already binge-watched my entire

Netflix list. It took me years to put show after show on there, and they all vanished in a week.'

Even through her nervous rambling, Erik seemed to pick up on what she was *really* trying to tell him. He crossed his arms in front of his chest, giving her an enticing view as they strained against the fabric of his shirt. The urge to trace the grooves of his muscles bubbled up in her, and Larissa swallowed hard.

His eyes flickered down to her throat, and that was enough to send a burst of liquid fire through her veins. When his gaze came back up to her, the blue of his eyes was darker. More intense. Daring her to get close enough to touch him.

'Let me show you something,' he said, his voice low enough that it vibrated over her skin, pushing the fire in her veins all the way to her core.

He stretched a hand out towards her, his fingers slightly curled in invitation. Larissa didn't have a choice but to slide her palm over his and let out a shaky breath when his hand closed around hers, tugging her to her feet and to a door at the other side of the office.

The door led to a small glass annex of the hospital. Larissa blinked when he flicked the lights on, her eyes adjusting to the sudden brightness. A worn-out couch and a few equally aged armchairs stood strewn around in no particular pattern, along with a bookshelf against the only non-glass wall of the building.

'This looks comfy,' she said, and Erik shrugged.

'It was designed as a greenhouse, but the light needed to run it during polar night was deemed too expensive. So now it's a little extra room that doesn't really get used outside of the long-term staff,' he replied.

'You wanted to show me another staff room?'

He shook his head, his eyes glancing at his wristwatch before coming back up to her. There was a spark of amusement in his gaze that sent a spray of warmth trickling down her spine. How on earth could he do that with just a glance?

'We haven't been at the hospital this late, and I just remembered that now is the perfect time to show you something. You probably already caught some glimpses of it, but this is quite the nice spot.' He still stood by the door, hand resting on the light switch. 'Are you ready?'

Larissa blinked. 'Ready for what?'

'I'll take that as a yes.' He grinned, then flipped the light switch, plunging them into darkness.

Except it wasn't dark. She could still make out Erik's shape, his pale skin glowing blue in the light of…the moon?

Larissa looked up and then gasped, her eyes going wide. Streaks of light green and blue interrupted the night sky, drowning out the moon and the stars with their own vibrant light. They pulsed in a steady wave, moving along the horizon as if they were sentient beings on a journey across the sky.

Larissa had seen glimpses of them, had even wondered if that was what she was really seeing. The northern lights.

They were even more breathtaking than any of the Instagram pictures she'd seen. Something about the vibrancy and the movement of the light just couldn't be captured by a camera.

Her eyes grew wider the longer she stared at the swirling ribbons of light, completely enthralled by beauty such as she'd never seen. 'Wow, this is…' Her voice trailed off as her words failed her. She'd seen glimpses of the northern lights on her way to the hotel, but they'd only ever been small fragments, disjointed. Not like this, where they unfurled across the sky in a celebration of colour and form.

'You get the best view of the lights after ten at night,' Erik said behind her, his voice right next to her ear.

She whirled around and there he was, standing right behind her, his face illuminated by the light of the aurora borealis. He'd stepped closer to her, only a hand span separating them, and Larissa tipped her head back to look him in the eyes. The sense of sudden proximity thundered through her, reminding her of what it had felt like when his fingers had wrapped around hers. Her touch-starved brain had extrapolated far too many scenarios from this small touch, all of them ending with their clothes on the floor of her room—or his house.

'I don't know what to say,' she breathed out, meaning both the lights and the intention she saw written in his gaze. Intention that rang through her like the chime of a bell, its vibrations winding her centre into a tight coil, ready to rupture. She swallowed the dryness in her mouth and almost whimpered when his eyes darted down to her throat again like a wild cat assessing its next move.

'We probably said enough,' he told her. Larissa didn't understand how his words were even remotely suggestive. On the surface they weren't, yet her knees shook. She nodded, not agreeing to what he had said, but to the gentle touch of his fingers as they skated up her arms until his fingertips rested on her neck.

Her heart leapt into her throat when Erik stepped forward. She was sure if she opened her mouth, her heart would leave her body entirely. His scent enveloped her, notes of pine and fresh fallen snow—a scent Larissa had only learned to really appreciate since coming here. It surrounded her whenever she stepped outside the hotel to get to work and reminded her so much of Erik that she wasn't sure she could ever think of anything else. Any*one* else.

A bolt of electricity went through her when the tip of his nose brushed against her, his face so near she could feel each breath skittering across her heated cheeks. Her eyes wanted to flutter closed so she could lose herself in this moment about to happen, but she didn't want to miss a single one of his movements, either.

'I don't know if this is a good idea,' he whispered, his mouth now so close to hers that the phantom of a kiss brushed over her lips. The fire inside her twisted at that, burning even higher. The need overrode any rational thought, any concerns about what-ifs melting away from just standing so close to Erik.

Instead of saying anything, Larissa slipped her hands up his back, pushing him even closer and sliding her mouth over his.

This kiss was a terrible idea. It was also the best idea Erik had ever had. The web of nerves winding through his body caught fire when Larissa's soft lips brushed over his. The singeing heat rendered him immobile for a heartbeat, unable to decide what his next move should be.

Then his body moved on its own, sliding his hands over her body and pressing her closer to him until their fronts were flush against each other. A shaky moan escaped her lips when his hand tangled into her hair, pulling back her head to deepen the kiss.

Her taste flooded his mouth, and it was exquisite. Exactly how he imagined she'd taste—and dear God, had he spent a lot of time daydreaming about this specific taste. About her and having her underneath him as she came undone.

The attraction clicking into place between them had been shocking from the first day. After everything had fallen apart around him and Astrid, he hadn't even contemplated anyone romantically. It just didn't work. Not when he'd dedicated his entire life to Svalbard and its community. Not when he had to be available 24/7 for any emergency pages or requests for medical attention. There were few such late-night requests, but they existed, and they were his responsibility. They would *always* come first, no matter the circumstances.

Only this wasn't romantic. They flirted and teased each other, but the conversation Larissa had with her friend said nothing about how to tell a guy about your feelings. She chose her words to fit her purpose, and that was physical. Larissa hadn't come here to start up a relationship with him when she would just end up leaving in a few weeks. No, she wanted something quick.

And all Erik wanted was her. Larissa.

He must have moaned her name, for she pulled her head back, looking at him with wide eyes. Her throat worked as she blinked. 'This is—' she began, and Erik cut her off by brushing another, softer kiss onto her lips.

'I think that's how you let a guy know,' he said when he drew back, earning himself another confused blink.

'What?'

'The answer to your friend's question. How you let a guy know you want to bang him. Pretty sure this is how you do it.'

Larissa's eyes went even wider, and the colour on her cheeks deepened enough that he could see it even under the blue light of the aurora borealis.

'And this is how you know he's interested, too,' he added as he slipped his hands into her hair and pulled her into another kiss. His tongue swept over her lips, and an involuntary groan left his throat when her taste clung to him again.

They were okay with just being in this moment, right? Should they talk about this? The last thing on Erik's mind was talking. Talking was for people who had things to figure out. They had nothing to figure out. No, this might actually be the most straightforward relationship in Erik's life.

The thoughts threatening to surface in his

mind drained out of him when Larissa dragged her hand across his abdomen until she reached his waistband. There she hovered, her fingers dancing over the material and grazing his flesh every now and then. A small touch, barely anything in the grand scheme of things, but it lit him on fire from the inside out.

A growl he had never heard from himself escaped his throat, and he hauled her closer to him, their breaths mingling as he deepened the kiss. He took several steps backward while keeping Larissa close to him until the backs of his knees collided with the couch behind him. Larissa yelped as she tumbled on top of him, and Erik grabbed her by the hips until she settled in his lap—straddling him.

Her heat pressed against his rising length, pushing against him and creating an ache that drove him out of his mind. If he'd had any reservations going into this, they were now all gone. He could focus on nothing but where her body connected with his and how he needed more.

Though apparently he was alone with this thought. For Larissa tore herself from his mouth, lips puffy from making out. 'This is not where I saw the evening going,' she huffed out, her eyes heavy-lidded as she looked down at him.

'Really? You were talking to your friend hoping it *wouldn't* end up like this?' he said just as breathlessly.

Larissa bent down with a chuckle, putting her forehead against his while wrapping both hands around his face. He marvelled at her lashes when her eyes fluttered shut. 'No, this is definitely where I *wanted* to end up. I just didn't realise that feelings were this mutual,' she said, eyes still closed.

Erik tightened his grip around her hips and moved against her, drawing out a deep moan from her. 'This is how mutual things are,' he growled, and he tilted his chin so he could capture her mouth again.

'And when I say feelings, I of course mean pants feelings,' she said as she untangled her mouth from his again. 'Like… horny feelings.'

Erik let out a dark chuckle and slipped his hand underneath the hem of her sweater, exposing her bare back to his touch. The feel of her smooth skin against his rough palm was pure ecstasy. He didn't mean to, but his hips bucked into her with the need for release already gathering at the base of his spine.

'We will keep it strictly to pants feelings.' He whispered the words against her skin as he nuzzled her neck, his other hand joining the one already exploring her back. His fingers slid higher and higher until they found the clasp of her bra.

A shaky breath left her mouth when he stopped there, and he sought out her eyes with his.

'This okay?' Erik's rough and low voice thundered through her like a lightning strike. Everything inside her buzzed, little fires erupting all over her body wherever she touched Erik. Her senses could make out nothing but him, where he touched her, how he smelled, how hard his body pressed against her—against the ache she needed him to satisfy.

Not in a million years would she have guessed that an inappropriate conversation with her best friend would lead her exactly to the position she wanted to be in. Erik was precisely the kind of distraction that she needed to make time in Svalbard go by faster. Especially since they both agreed on what this was supposed to be.

So she nodded, and a shiver crawled down her spine when the tension of her bra loosened around her chest. Erik pushed up the sweater, exposing her flesh to the chilly air as he pulled both items of clothing away from her. Her breath came out in a stutter when he leaned back, sinking further into the couch. His eyes roamed over her, drinking her in, and the rise and fall of his chest increased.

They were still, each one staring at the other. Then, ever so slowly, Erik traced his hand from her back over her ribs to her front, fingertips brushing against the underside of her breast. Her shaky breath turned into a gasp when he palmed her, squeezing softly. A word she couldn't understand slipped from him as he brushed his thumb over her taut nipple. Her back arched, pushing further into his touch, and the low groan filling the space between them set every nerve in her body on fire.

'What?' she asked, her words no more than a whisper.

Erik's gaze snapped up to her, the passion glazing his eyes drawing out a whimper of need. He blinked twice, as if he needed time to parse her question. 'What do you mean?'

'You said…' He didn't give her enough time to verbalise her thoughts. Larissa shuddered, breaking out in full-body goose flesh when his lips connected with the skin between her breasts. His tongue darted out, caressing her and creating a stark contrast between his warmth and the chill of the night air.

This was really happening. Her plan had been to treat herself to overly expensive strawberries and shut herself in her room for the entire weekend. Because the heat between them had already been climbing with each encounter, and what she had thought she desperately needed was a few days away from him so she could reset.

But there was no resetting this. Not as Erik closed his lips around her nipple, drawing it into his mouth and circling her tip with his tongue until her vision blurred.

She let out a pant, one that she knew would normally embarrass her. Who panted like that on a featherlight touch? It wasn't like this was the first time anyone touched her like that. Except somehow it was. Something about the tenderness, the feverish glaze of his eyes as he looked up at her, threatened to undo Larissa before they had even shed all of their clothes.

Erik nuzzled the skin between her breasts again, his breath hot on her as he traced his lips down her stomach. Each lick of his tongue sent sparks flying from wherever he was touching her straight to her core—right where she ached for his touch.

Larissa clawed at his shirt, dragging the fabric up his back until her fingertips brushed over his skin, relishing the smooth warmth that met her there. Lean muscles worked under her fingers as he drew the shirt over his head. Larissa leaned back, drinking all of him in.

The blue-green light filtering through the glass roof bathed them, illuminating his skin in a similar glow to that surrounding them—as if someone had crafted him out of the northern lights. His broad chest moved up and down at a fast pace and increased when Larissa reached her hand out, tracing the hard lines of each pec. She shivered when she ran her fingers through his chest hair, following the trail down—all the way to his trousers. Larissa paused there, raising her gaze to his. Then she slipped two fingers underneath his waistband, brushing over the top of his straining manhood.

Another Norwegian word left his lips through tightly shut teeth, the hiss that followed one of pure arousal. She didn't need to understand the language to know what was happening—what the tiny words meant that he couldn't help but utter in his native tongue.

'Your trousers seem a bit tight,' she said, hardly recognising her own voice. It was so low, filled with a longing that she hadn't known she possessed within her. It wasn't like she hadn't enjoyed sex or intimacy outside of her one serious relationship. She had. Enough times that she knew what she liked and what she didn't like to get a quick release.

This should also be just a quick release and nothing more. A fling between two colleagues who, at the end of her contract, would become strangers again. Except they hadn't done more than kiss—*for the first time today*—and Larissa was already burning for more.

Erik huffed a laugh, his big hands coming to

rest on each side of her hips, his gaze heavy-lidded. 'This wasn't how I saw this evening going,' he said, each word accompanied by a deep breath.

'You eavesdropped on my conversation, invited me to drinks with you and didn't think that it would end in sex?' He didn't need to know that she hadn't believed that, either. Had thought she was making up this attraction zipping between them. She was so rusty in the seduction game that she had to ask Ally how to let him know what she wanted. Never mind that she had ended up not needing any help, after all.

'Well, I…' The last word morphed into a choked sound when Larissa undid the button of his trousers with one flick of her finger, the back of her hand pressing against his length. 'The hook up culture isn't exactly thriving here.'

Larissa pulled down his trousers' zipper, folding the fabric to the side. His erection strained against his underwear, and her thighs clenched at the sight. Dear God, it had been far too long since she'd actually had a good orgasm that hadn't been her own handiwork.

'I can imagine it's far too easy to fall into a relationship dynamic if you have the choice out of three people,' she replied, her eyes fixed on him. His right hand still clung to her hip while his left one wandered to her front, drawing tiny circles on her skin as he went all the way to her waistband—repeating what she had done to him until his hand had access to where she wanted him to be. His fingers brushed over the apex of her thighs, sending a renewed shower of pure fire through her, making her jerk forward. She slid back on his thighs and braced her hands on his knees to bare herself more—give him access to what they both wanted.

The sound leaving Erik's throat could only be described as a growl. It skittered across her skin, igniting her from the inside out, just as his fingers swept over the elastic band of her underwear. He played with it for a few seconds, each touch slow and torturous as it ratcheted up the arousal within her. Then his fingers slipped over the fabric of her underwear and pushed down where the ache was the greatest.

Her fingers clenched around his knees. Her hips jerked, leaning into his touch as if his fingers were the only ones who could satisfy her. As if it was Erik—and not sex in general—that brought her this pleasure.

'*Faen*, Larissa…you are already soaked for me,' he whispered, his breath shaky as he exhaled. Larissa's inner walls clenched at the words, at the *need* for him to finally touch her.

Her breaths came in rapid bursts as his fingers kept working her through the fabric, teasing her with a phantom of what his touch could be like without any barrier between them—and keeping her release just outside of her grasp.

Gathering some hard-fought breath into her lungs, she bit out, 'Are we going to do this or what?'

They were fighting words, meant to challenge him as well as make it absolutely clear what she wanted—some low-stakes sex between two consenting adults.

Erik clicked his tongue, his thumb still brushing over her. 'I've been looking forward to this since the day you arrived,' he said, and leaned forward to brush his tongue against her nipple. 'I'm going to enjoy you.'

His voice was deep and filled with a promise of release that had her straining against his hand between her thighs. Had anyone ever said something this *hot* to her? If they had, Larissa had no recollection of it. She was at the point where she was certain no one had even touched her properly, because she would remember such an intense burn in her core. Would have sought it out if she'd known just how good it could be.

'I'm still around for six more weeks,' she huffed out. 'Plenty of time to enjoy me.'

His hand stilled. Had he thought of this as a one-time thing? Granted, they hadn't spoken about *any* of this at all, so Larissa had just blurted out what she wanted—a fling for the duration of her stay. She pushed off his knees, wanting to slide closer and look at him when his grip around her hip tightened.

'Then I guess I can take my time to learn what drives you wild,' he said. His fingers slipped beneath the waistband of her underwear.

Her mind emptied of any thoughts. Pure pleasure lanced through her, her body responding to the featherlight touch. Apparently, he didn't need to learn what drove her wild, because this was it.

'Right there,' she breathed out to underline the thoughts in her head.

Erik obliged, running his finger up and down her centre. Release gathered around her like an iridescent veil—ready to shatter. Her back bowed into his touch, and she completely shattered when his hot breath skated over her skin and his mouth closed around her nipple again. He didn't stop, kept drawing longer and lazier circles as the tension flowed out of her body. When she slumped forward, he wrapped his arms around her, holding her close. Her chest heaved big breaths as Larissa gathered herself from the edges of space where Erik's touch had put her. After she finally reached her own body again, a fresh wave of arousal crashed through her when his erection pressed against her.

A smile spread over her lips as she ground against him, and Erik let out a loud hiss, his head falling back against the couch. 'Sounds like we are both easy to figure out,' Larissa whispered against his ear as she flexed her hips again. Her mouth pressed against his and swallowed Erik's second groan.

Then she slipped off his lap, kneeling down in front of him—between his legs. She reached up to pull his trousers down when his hand wrapped around her wrist.

'I wouldn't offer if I didn't…' she began, but her voice trailed off when Erik's head tilted sideways, his eyes on the door.

Larissa flinched when he jumped to his feet, pulling his trousers back up as he did. 'Someone is coming,' he said, grabbing the pile of clothes on the floor and throwing her sweater—sans bra—at her. Then he pulled his own shirt over his head, and Larissa buttoned her trousers.

The second she patted down the hem of her sweater, the door swung open with a tentative 'Erik?' from a female voice. The lights flickered above them before turning on, and Larissa winced at the sudden brightness, closing her eyes.

'I came to check on Daniela, and she told me— Why are you sitting in the dark?' Ingrid's voice filled the room.

Larissa didn't know what to say, hadn't even realised how easily accessible this part of the hospital was to anyone else. To think she had been about to…

'I was showing Larissa the aurora borealis,' Erik said, his words clipped. Apparently he wasn't happy about the interruption, either. 'Do you need me for something?'

'Yes, her mother asked me to bring over some of her things, and she's complaining about pain,' Ingrid said. Larissa had to blink a few more times before her eyes adjusted to the sudden brightness. When they did, she looked at the receptionist and gave her a tentative smile. The old woman didn't return it. Instead, her sharp gaze flicked between her and Erik, the line between her brows growing deeper.

Erik seemed to notice her inquisitive stare too, for he stepped towards Ingrid, grabbing her attention and ushering her out of the room. Larissa caught a few snippets of their hushed discussion in Norwegian before the door closed, leaving her alone in the annex.

CHAPTER SEVEN

'So, HE FINGERED YOU, and then he just hasn't said anything ever since?' Ally asked in her ear, and even though Larissa was well used to her best friend's preferred language, she still cringed. Something about reducing what happened between her and Erik to *fingering* just felt wrong. Even though it really was what had happened.

Larissa had got home from another day of work half an hour ago to call Ally. Larissa had opened up about that night under the northern lights.

'Oh my God, can I see it?' Those had been the first words about all of this from Ally. Because Larissa couldn't deny her anything, she'd got dressed while they spoke and was now close to the otherwise dark hospital. She didn't see any of the lights, but it was still early. She'd hang out on that cursed couch, wondering where she went wrong that everything between her and Erik had run so off the rails, while Ally assured her it had nothing to do with her. That seemed like an evening spent well.

'Can we go back to talking about your close encounter in a dank cave? That seems more urgent,' Larissa said, suddenly unsure if she wanted to speak about Erik.

'Um, no. I was still clothed for that, so by hierarchy of nudeness, your topic is more pressing.' She said it as if the hierarchy of nudeness was a real concept.

Ugh, fine. She might as well get it over with. 'We haven't really spoken ever since this thing a week ago—which is weird. Even if we didn't work together, we kind of just…hung out?' Larissa said, burying her face in her scarf to ward off the chilly wind blowing across her. 'He probably regrets getting so close after I told him he would have weeks to enjoy me.' That memory summoned another cringe. Why was it that whenever she thought she was being some sort of sexy siren, she actually felt more like a hag who had never in her life learned how to flirt? Or was her total inexperience in casual flings showing? Until Rachel, she'd never seen anyone beyond one night.

She pushed thoughts of Rachel away the second they popped up, not letting them take root in her head. Nothing good could come of thinking about her.

'Maybe he's busy. Did you guys text much before all of this?' Ally asked, her voice a low hush. Probably to avoid waking anyone up. It was well past the evening hours for her.

'Not really? We hung out in the hospital, kind of just doing our own thing but…together? We had some morning walks where we would talk, but with Martin back on his feet, I'm no longer needed for dog walking duties.' It was strange—and concerning—how much she missed those morning walks. Larissa had thought she would be glad to sleep in a few more hours before her shift at the hospital, but as if to remind her something was missing, her body woke her up every morning to get ready. Now she spent her morning sitting downstairs, having coffee by the fire and scrolling through her phone until it was time to leave. Sometimes locals joined her for a coffee, knowing the hotel was the earliest place where they could buy it, and asked her about her time in Svalbard.

Those were the mornings Larissa enjoyed the most, filling her with a warm sense of something she couldn't name.

'You should start texting him. Set the precedent so he can follow it,' Ally said, and Larissa knew how desperate she was to talk to Erik, because she was considering her suggestion. Should she just message him? At this point, she was all but convinced that Erik was avoiding her. The only reason she could come up with for that avoidance was how deep the regret of what happened between them sat within him. How he wanted to just forget she'd ever existed. So much that he'd literally started working different hours. Larissa now worked at the same time as one of the more experienced nurses taking appointments that didn't need to be seen by a doctor.

It reminded her so much of how she and Ally had run their clinic that her heart ached inside her chest with longing for a time that was now forever gone.

'Isn't that like super desperate? I'm down for some fun, but I won't chase him if he doesn't want…well, me.' The words didn't feel right on her tongue, though she couldn't pinpoint why. Of course he didn't want *her*. That implied an emotional connection that far exceeded what they had. They were just attracted to each other.

'Mmm, you're right. Damn.' Ally hummed in her ear, and then she went on to present her next idea. Only Larissa didn't hear it. As she approached the front of the hospital, the door swung open, and Erik stepped out with a box under one arm and a duffel bag slung over the other.

She froze in her steps, staring at the man who had been eluding her for the better part of an entire week. The proof that he had indeed begun working late nights for the past week just to avoid her stung a lot more than she was willing to admit.

'Ally, I have to go,' Larissa whispered and heard rustling from the other side of the phone line as her friend sat up.

'What's going on?' she asked, her tone a lot more alert than it had been a few moments ago.

'Erik just walked out of the hospital.'

'Seriously?'

'Yes, seriously. What kind of question is that?' Larissa hissed, staring the figure down. He walked over to a parked car, opening the back and putting the box and duffel inside. He hadn't spotted her yet, but the moment he turned around, he would see her standing there, looking at him like some deranged stalker.

'I'll have to show you the northern lights later,' she said, and held her breath when Erik moved again, turning around to head back into the clinic. He turned fully, his eyes gliding over her, and Larissa thought maybe he hadn't seen her or thought she was just a pedestrian out on a stroll. But then he did a double-take, his head whipping back to her and staring across the distance. His head tipped slightly to the side, scanning her. Then he moved towards her.

'He's coming to talk to me,' she said, unsure

why her heart was beating faster. 'Ally, hang up the phone.'

'What? Why do I have to hang up?'

'Because my phone is three layers down. I can't reach it.'

Ally made a whining noise. 'What if I'm really quiet?'

'Ally!'

'Fine, fine. Jeez. I expect an update at the first convenient moment.' The line went quiet as Ally hung up just in time for Erik to reach her.

He stopped a few paces away from her, his head still slightly tilted, as if she was some piece of art he needed to study from different angles to understand it.

'What are you doing here?' he asked, taking another step closer.

Larissa crossed her arms in front of her. 'I work here.'

She could see Erik's brows narrow. She knew that behind the scarf, there was a frown tugging at his lips. If that was how he was going to play it, she was more than happy to comply.

'Not at this hour,' he said, exactly how she'd hoped he would.

'Well, neither do you. Yet here you are with your mystery box and mystery…duffel bag.' She swallowed, unsure if the jab had landed as intended. Her words sounded more petulant than fierce in her ears, but she'd committed to this, so there was no going back.

Across the distance, she heard Erik snort. 'This is my hospital. I have to work whenever there's work. Sometimes that means moving mystery objects around, yes. I'll concede this much.'

Larissa's temper flared at the ease in his tone, the relaxed posture. If she hadn't known better, she could have sworn that he didn't have a single clue they hadn't seen each other in about a week. Was he *that* indifferent about her? He didn't even notice her absence when he was working different shifts? So much that joking around seemed appropriate? Maybe she really had misjudged the friendship they had developed over the early morning dog walks.

The thought stung despite her best attempts to not let it bother her.

Instead, she nodded towards the car. 'I've never seen you drive a car before,' she said, attempting to bring some kind of normalcy between them again. Why had she somehow forgotten how to talk to him? Oh right, because last time they had said anything to each other, he'd told her in how many different ways he would enjoy her for the next few weeks. That had been right before he'd vanished for the better part of a week.

'I have to go vaccinate some new arrivals at a research facility a few hours away.'

That caught Larissa's attention. 'What vaccine do people need when they arrive here?' she asked, her brow furrowed. She hadn't received any special vaccine upon arrival.

She heard Erik chuckle again, and she tried to hang on to her indignation as the sound vibrated through the night air and settled down in her core, warming her from the inside out.

'The yearly flu vaccine.'

Larissa blinked at him. 'The flu vaccine? You have to drive all the way there just to give them a vaccine?'

'Hey now, don't downplay the importance of the flu vaccine. They live in close quarters with each other, heightening the chance that if one person gets it, the others will catch it, too,' he said, and though his words were an admonishment, there was an amused twinkle in his eyes. It was the latter that drove her temper into a hotter territory.

'I know how important the flu vaccine is. You can't even imagine how much time I've spent sending my patients annoying emails and texts about the benefits and why they should come in and get their free jab. But isn't...'

Her voice trailed off as her thoughts stalled and she questioned her own knowledge of the situation.

Erik raised an eyebrow, the corner of his lip twitching. 'Isn't what?'

'Isn't it all ice here? If they don't leave the research centre, how would they even contract anything?' Of course, germs and bacteria could survive the ice in the right circumstances, but it didn't seem as likely.

'Ah, I see. It's mostly a precaution, but some of them come to Longyearbyen and mingle with locals and tourists. I go there every six months to do a physical and deliver any medicine they need and also some other things they asked for.' His eyes darted to the box he'd just put in the car. When she followed his gaze, she could see there were already other boxes in there.

'How far is the research centre?' she asked, as an idea began to gnaw at her.

'It's a three-hour drive, but it will take me most of the night and some of the day to get through everyone's physical. I probably won't be back until later tomorrow.' Erik shrugged, and she wasn't sure why he was telling her this. It wasn't like he had kept her abreast of his schedule this entire week and if he hadn't just presented her with a solid reason he needed to leave, she would have accused him of avoiding her.

He probably *was* avoiding her, anyway. So this was the best opportunity she had to figure out what went wrong between them. With her decision solidifying in her mind, Larissa stepped around Erik and walked over to the passenger door of the car.

Erik was there a heartbeat later, his hand coming down on the window and holding the door closed. 'What are you doing?'

'I'm coming with you. If it'll take you all night to vaccinate and examine people, then one additional person should cut that in half,' she insisted, determined not to let him brush her off.

'It's not necessary. I can handle it by myself.'

'I know you can. And I'm telling you that you don't have to. I'm here to help. That's literally why I came to Svalbard.'

His eyes narrowed on her, but Larissa didn't back off, her hand still on the door handle. 'What if there's something needed at the hospital that requires a doctor?' he asked.

'It's Saturday tomorrow. There are no scheduled appointments, and Melanie is on call for any walk-ins that can be handled by a nurse. If anything minor comes through the door, Melanie will take care of it, while the major things will be stabilised and pushed to Tromsø. Though I highly doubt that tomorrow is the day when something catastrophic happens.' There hadn't been a single incident where they needed to call the medevac to transport someone to mainland Norway in the three weeks she'd been here. Sometimes she didn't even have an entire day full of people to see and instead passed her time by scrolling through her phone and sending Ally pictures of herself in random places in the hospital with the caption, 'Look at me having all of this adventure we talked about.'

'I…' Erik stalled, clearly looking for another excuse to push her away.

So she went on, 'Listen, I know after what happened the other night, we haven't really seen each other. I think we should…talk about it. I'm not asking for anything else. But we're still colleagues, so I'd rather figure it out before the next month gets super awkward.' She chuckled as she added, 'I can't run away again, even though that's my preferred way, so I guess I have to be mature about it.'

Erik huffed a laugh, clouds of condensation billowing up in the space between them. 'You're right,' he said with a sigh. Even though she had told herself that the outcome of the conversation didn't matter to her, something sharp wedged itself between her ribs at his sigh. In her mind, she had nursed the hope that he might have just been busy and that he hadn't been avoiding her. But the pained concession she'd just wrung from him confirmed he had.

He regretted what happened between them.

'We'll have to work through the night, though.

The researchers were kind enough to adjust their schedule so we can keep the time away from the hospital to a minimum,' he said, and released his grip on the door.

He agreed they needed to talk. His tactic of avoiding Larissa had only brought him to the end of the week before she'd caught up with him. Erik really didn't know what he had expected. He'd known eventually everything would catch up to him, and he needed to make a decision. That was the tricky part—the thing that made him avoid her like some conflict-averse child. Because he knew very well what he wanted. That was the problem. He couldn't forget the night he had shown her the northern lights. Every time he closed his eyes, he could see her sitting on his lap, her hips moving against his fingers as he brought her to climax. How easy it had been, how right it had felt. Like he knew this woman inside out and what made her tick. What made her come.

Only that was, of course, nonsense. Erik knew so little about Larissa except the details she'd shared with him on their dog walks and the conversation they'd had in the pub. Though they saw each other at the hospital, their relationship existed mostly in companionable silence.

The tension snapping in place between them was palpable, enveloping everything around them as they sat in the car on their way to the research outpost northwards. They said they would talk, and that was Erik's intention. Only he did not know where to even start. He hadn't made up his own mind. The cautious part within him urged him to forget that one night had ever happened, that they couldn't go there again, no matter how temporary it would be. But then he remembered the feel of her around his fingers, how sweet her mouth tasted on his, and he couldn't give that up just yet.

From the corner of his eye, he saw Larissa's mane of curls bob, as if she was shaking her head. Then her strained laughter filled the air. He glanced at her before turning his head back to the road. 'What?' he asked when she continued to chuckle.

'I don't think we've ever been this tense before.'

Erik shrugged, trying his best to ignore the apparently quite obvious tension in his shoulders as he said, 'I'm not tense.'

'Um, yeah you are. I've known you for close to a month now, and in that time, you have remained unfazed. Up until this moment. Now that I know you better, you can't convince me otherwise.' She crossed her arms in front of her chest, levelling a stare at him. 'What's on your mind?'

Now that I know you better. Those words

should have sent alarm bells ringing through him, urging him to pull the emergency brakes. They didn't need to know each other to work together. They didn't even need to know each other to have sex. It was probably better if they didn't. But although he understood all of this, the words still sparked a warmth inside his chest that radiated through his entire body.

He had no idea why he responded. Maybe because she might leave, or maybe because something about showing her another slice of him just felt right. 'It's been a while since I let anyone this close, and I get that what happened between us is just physical, but I guess—I'm comfortable by myself. And to the annoyance of my parents, I don't have the need to find anyone to have in my life permanently. My job is that thing for me. Svalbard holds that place in my heart.'

He paused, sorting through his thoughts to figure out what he wanted to say. Breathing out a sigh, he continued, 'I told you I knew what it was like to have my heart broken. When that happened to me, my parents had got themselves far too involved with my ex. She bridged some of the gap between us by getting involved in the hotel business, and they thought I finally found my missing piece.'

Erik looked straight ahead, watching the snow drift through the air as the tyres disrupted the powdery ice on the ground. 'I don't believe there is a missing piece. What they think is missing is just occupied by something other than romantic love. It's represented in that need inside of me to help my community.' He paused, daring a glance at her to see if she understood what he meant. If she had felt this specific thing inside her, too.

A small smile appeared on her lips, and she nodded. 'A calling. The compulsion to do the work that we do.'

He nodded, surprised that someone finally understood. That she specifically understood. Erik couldn't point towards the reason why, but having her understanding set his stomach on a freefall.

'Familial obligations are a strange thing to navigate,' Larissa said, her tone wistful, and he turned his head again.

'You had them even though you basically raised yourself?' he asked, remembering the things she'd shared with him—and part of the reason he had let her see as much of him as he had.

'Mmm, I don't know.' She hummed, shifting in her seat again so she faced the window. Her hand came down on the glass, her fingers tracing what he assumed were the flurries of snow outside. Quiet settled in between them, underpinned by the steady rumbling of the car's engine. His eyes flickered to the clock on the dashboard and widened when he saw the time. They had already been driving for two and a half hours. Another half an hour and they would be at their destination.

'My parents only paid me attention when I got to my third year in med school, when things looked more serious. They were never really interested in anything I did if it didn't affect them. So their daughter suddenly being halfway through to becoming a physician suddenly caught their attention,' Larissa said, just as he thought her previous answer was all he would get.

'By that point, I didn't care anymore. Life by myself was just simpler to navigate. I already knew how to ensure I ate, slept and had clean laundry for school. That didn't change when I left my family home behind to go to med school. If I'm being honest, it probably helped me in some aspects. The only thing I'm unsure about is whether an eleven-year-old should need to learn these skills in the first place. But here we are.'

Larissa shared the struggles of her upbringing a lot more freely than he'd expected anyone carrying these things around with them would. Then again, he sensed something beneath all of that—something she kept close to her chest. Something that still hurt, unlike what had happened with her parents. Erik knew that because he was the same. And precisely for that reason, he knew he shouldn't go digging for it. They would be better off in the long run if he let the things inside her be. If he shared nothing from inside himself, either.

'And yet here you are, on the run from a heartbreak someone inflicted on you even though you learned to guard yourself so well.' The words struck him, even though he wasn't the target—even though *he* had said them. They were intended to get through to her, to show her he saw what was happening and that he understood.

Larissa's hand froze on the glass, then dropped slowly as she turned around to look at him. Then her eyes darted to where the vague shape of a building coalesced on the horizon. Wind whipped around them, far stronger than when they'd departed from Longyearbyen, obscuring some of the view ahead of them.

'Guess at least now I know what to avoid. You won't catch me being dumb enough to fall for someone.' He knew the tone in her voice all too well—the icy barb warning anyone from getting too close. In so many aspects, they were similar to each other. How could it have happened that they got so close without them even noticing? Of course Erik had realised his attraction to her the first day they'd met, and promptly kept his distance as much as possible while working with her. That vow lasted less than a day before he found her in his office and close enough that he could smell the fragrance of flowers she left in her wake.

'I don't intend this as criticism but rather an observation. The reason I didn't speak to you this week was that I needed to think about what happened and how it fits into everything I know about you,' he said, getting to the underlying point of his tension. They would work through the night, and it would turn out far too long if he didn't get this out now—even though a part of him wanted to forget it had ever happened. Because the craving flickering inside him burned far too bright already.

She remained quiet as they watched the building on the horizon grow taller. Then Larissa said, 'So, what do you want to do now? I'm not sure what it means when a guy tells me he would like to use the next four weeks to figure out what drives me wild just for him to spend an entire week ignoring me. Are you lacking clarity?'

Her words were blunt. Under any other circumstances, Erik knew he would have felt a stab of guilt. He probably did, except the need flaring hot and searing within him covered up his other emotions, burning away anything else that might have attempted to compete with this feeling inside of him.

'A lack of clarity is a good starting point. What

I'm worried about is closeness.' He was already slipping down that path, scared of it enough that he'd retreated from her this week. It hadn't been the most mature thing to do, but he needed time to figure her out. Figure himself out.

Steering right, Erik left what little he could see of the main road and took the small snowy path to the research building. He pulled into an open parking bay, casting his eyes around. There were three more cars around them. Larissa seemed to notice as well, looking up at the building before her eyes landed on Erik. A shiver clawed through him as those brown eyes narrowed on him and visions of that night a week ago filled his mind. He knew exactly what her face looked like when she stood too close to the edge, how her breathing turned ragged and fast, panting until—

'You mean you are worried about feelings entering this?' He focused on the present, on the conversation they needed to have. Even though when he was this close to her, he wanted to do many things to her, and none of them involved much talking.

'That's...' His voice trailed off as he searched for the truth inside him. 'You asked me if I ever had my heart broken hard enough that I just needed to be elsewhere. I said I have, and my elsewhere is my work. My purpose in this community. There isn't much space for anything else outside of that. Even my family gave way.'

Erik couldn't tell what thoughts were rolling around behind her eyes. He kept staring at her, searching her expression for something to latch on to. Eventually, she shook her head, but a smile tugged at her lips. 'If we agree that this is what we want, then we should be fine. Just some fun while I'm here with no risks of getting attached. I'm down for that if you are.'

How was this simultaneously the answer he wanted and had feared? Because there was no way in hell he could say no to her. Not when he'd already had her above him, sighing his name as she clenched around his fingers. That was a sight he knew he would never tire of—which was why he feared slipping in too deep. He was already burning on the inside with the need to touch her.

His voice was rough when he said, 'I want things between us to be clear. My life is here, and nothing is going to change that.'

He'd not told her about Astrid—at least not in detail. But Erik wasn't naive. He knew that even if they went into this with the best intentions, things could happen. People developed feelings even when they swore they wouldn't. So he needed to be clear about where he stood so that even if something were to happen, his stance was crystal clear from the very beginning.

'I'm not planning on whisking you away to England by the end of my stint here. But I am planning on leaving.' She paused, her eyes drifting down to where his hand still gripped the gearshift. Slowly, she extended her hand, covering his with hers and prying his fingers open. When their hands intertwined, she looked back up at him and said, 'Let's make it clear what we want by discussing what happened in the past.'

Erik blinked, his head tilted to the side. 'What do you mean?'

Her hand squeezed his as she took a deep breath. 'I was happy to live my life alone—the way I had always done. Casual, one-night things were all I needed. Men more often than women because of how male-dominated the medical field is. Then I met Rachel, and she seemed to get me. She wouldn't complain when I spent hours at the clinic or if I was too tired to do something. It felt like she was trying her best to fit into the life I already had, so when things became more serious, she had helpful solutions at hand.' She raised her free hand, making air quotes around the word 'helpful'. 'Things like, "What if I moved in with you? That way it doesn't matter how late you come home." And because I saw her compromise, I thought I needed to do that, too. My parents had never compromised with each other, and their fights dragged out for days. I didn't want that in my life.'

Her voice was even, hardly betraying the emotional depth her words laid bare. Or was it because of the lack of any inflection in her voice that he could tell how deep this wound still ran? Erik remained quiet, not wanting to disrupt the moment building between them.

'Turns out all the helpful things she did were for the purpose of getting concessions out of me. She thought she could drag me over to her side if I let her come close enough. Even though she had said she understood my hours, soon came the snide remarks and the passive-aggressive cold dinner left on the table. I thought we had agreed on who we wanted to be together, but she changed her mind—and tried to force that change on me. And when I didn't change fast enough, she sought out other people while still pretending to be with me. Like the efforts I made for her were not enough to be loved or valued. I, once again, became secondary to her needs.'

His eyes widened as he realised the meaning of her earlier words. Sharing not necessarily for the sake of getting to know each other better, but to avoid the things that were still haunting them. He knew she had her own life—just like he had his—and that was the common ground they could meet on.

'Our stories are strangely similar,' he said, each word coming to him haltingly. Erik had never fully opened up about his struggles with Astrid. Who would he even have to talk to? His parents were too obsessed with the next person to enter his life. Too keen on recreating what they thought to be the ultimate goal in life: to find your other half.

His eyes drifted to Larissa, who still held his hand wrapped in hers. Maybe that was a second thing they could do for each other. Hold space when they didn't have anyone to do that for them in their real lives. This wasn't real, so they could make up the rules as they wanted.

'Astrid came to Svalbard the way most people outside of tourists do. They are either looking for something or running away. She was the former, looking for something else in life. Something to fulfil her. She landed in my hospital on her second night in Longyearbyen with potential frostbite, and we just…clicked. I'd been so focused on my work for so long at this point that I didn't understand her interest in me until my sister pointed it out.' As time passed, it got harder to remember the reasons why he'd fallen for his ex-fiancée. The hurt had overwritten almost all of his memories of her, and when he'd moved on from the pain, little else to remind him of her remained.

But he could understand Larissa better now,

knowing what she had told him. Could let him-self sink a bit deeper into the thing that was their attraction without getting lost in it. Because he knew it was a dead end. She needed to know that about him, too.

'She stayed at the Aurora Hotel. After she left the hospital, I went there a few times for fol-low-up appointments, and I think what drew me in was how she could talk to me in a way that made me feel seen and understood—and, at the same time, do the same with my parents. She brought us into the same room, interacting with each other without even trying.'

A gust of wind rattled the windows, obscur-ing their vision with a flurry of snow. Laris-sa's eyes widened as even the building right in front of them became hazy with the ice rising around them. Something inside Erik shifted as he looked outside. Beyond the exterior lights from the building, he couldn't actually *see* anything, but his senses still picked up on something. A sixth sense he'd developed from years of living surrounded by snow and ice.

'We should go inside. I think there's a storm coming,' he said, even though a part of him hes-itated to end their conversation prematurely. By the set of Larissa's jaw when he said that, he could tell that she didn't want to move either.

So he added, 'I will tell you everything once

we're settled inside and have seen to the researchers. Okay?'

Her eyes narrowed at him, and he couldn't blame her. Whatever was happening between them was fresh. Fragile. He'd already tested the stability by ignoring her for a week straight. But then she nodded, and they worked in tandem to pick up everything from the car and hurry inside the building. Erik's sixth sense proved accurate, because hours later, as they neared completing their work, the storm still hadn't abated—and they wouldn't be leaving until it did.

CHAPTER EIGHT

'WHAT DO YOU do during your time off?' Larissa pressed the cotton ball against the tiny puncture wound the needle left on the researcher's arm, giving it a good squeeze to encourage the platelets to do their job before she slapped a plaster on it.

The researcher, Elsie, shrugged, as if no one had ever asked her that question. A common reaction, Larissa found, as she had asked every person who walked through that door and they all had a variation of a shrug, a contemplative scowl or just a shake of their heads.

'We have downtime if we want it, but I usually spend time in the lab anyway,' she said, her lips pulled into a frown. 'But now that I say it out loud, it sounds sad. Like I'm just spending my days in this building, looking at spreadsheets of different readings.'

Larissa chuckled at that. After securing the plaster to Elsie's skin, she grabbed the blood pressure cuff and wound it around the woman's upper arm, pressing on the mechanism to inflate it and holding the stethoscope against the crook of Elsie's arm.

'I always wondered how that works,' Elsie said when the cuff was fully deflated. The sound of Velcro filled the air as she took it off, setting it aside and noting down the blood pressure on the patient chart Erik had provided her.

She looked up from the piece of paper. 'How what works?'

'Measuring blood pressure with a stethoscope like that.'

'Oh…' Larissa's eyes darted towards the blood pressure cuff she had discarded on the worktable behind her. 'You know how your blood pressure comprises two numbers?'

Elsie nodded, and she continued, 'The first one is the systolic blood pressure—that's the pressure when the heart is beating. I slowly release the pressure on the cuff while listening for a whooshing or thumping sound. It's the pressure at which your blood flows again in the artery as the cuff pressure lowers.'

She picked up the pen, pointing at the numbers she'd written down. 'The other number is the diastolic pressure, which is the one in the arteries when the heart rests between beats. I figure that one out by deflating the cuff further and waiting for the sound to stop.'

Raising her hand, she tapped the point of the pen against the gauge on the cuff lying on the table. 'Then it's just a matter of writing the numbers down.'

Elsie looked at her with an appreciative smile. 'You did it so fast.'

It was Larissa's turn to shrug. 'I've done this more times than I can count. Now I don't even have to think about it anymore. I'm sure there are aspects of your work that are similar.'

The woman nodded, her eyes glazing over slightly as if she was diving for a specific memory to match it against what she had just heard. As much as Larissa enjoyed the people she'd met here, she couldn't listen to another science story without rolling her eyes. So before Elsie could say anything, she got to her feet, signalling that the examination was over.

'And that's you done with a clean bill of health,' Larissa said as she finished her notes, returning the smile Elsie gave her.

The woman waved as she opened the door and closed it behind her, leaving Larissa alone with her thoughts. Again. The regret of ushering the woman out as fast as she had whooshed through her. She contemplated how weird it would be if she ran after her, asking her what kinds of things had become second nature to her as she spent her days here at the research centre looking at snow. Or whatever else they did here.

Larissa's fried brain genuinely couldn't retain any information that wasn't medically relevant. But pretending to listen helped her ignore the mounting unease in her belly at what she had done in the car. How much of herself she had just put out there for everyone to see. And by everyone, she obviously meant Erik, though as far as Svalbard was concerned, he was already an enormous part of *everyone*.

Not for the first time since they had divided up the researchers to do their health checks, Larissa picked up her phone. Still zero bars. There was a Wi-Fi network attached to the research centre, but she'd felt too awkward to ask anyone for the password. *What colour was the urine you passed last? Oh, and also, what's the Wi-Fi password?*

She'd have to freak out at Ally later, which was totally fine. She was a functioning adult who didn't need her best friend to help her process her feelings. Larissa was a *doctor*, telling people all day about their health, both physically and mentally. Why was the thought of facing Erik after she had told him about Rachel so daunting?

Larissa didn't even know what had possessed her. For the most part, she had meant what she'd said. He'd been avoiding her because of some notion that his touch might have warped her brain enough for her to catch feelings for him. If the roles were reversed, she probably would have had the same concern. And because she didn't want him to keep having those thoughts, she shared what had happened between her and Rachel. Had let him into the ruins that this relationship had left in her.

But another part of her had wanted him to know because… That was the part that had her freaking out. Because she simply wanted him to know her. Wanted him to have a piece of her, even though all she had said to him pointed in the other direction.

A knock sounded on the door, and a second later, the cause of all her jumbled thoughts walked through it. Erik crossed half of the room before he stopped. She thought she spotted something akin to worry in his expression, but when he raised his eyes to look at her, she took in a sharp breath. His smouldering gaze heated the air between them, emptying her brain of any thoughts that had kept her spinning a few seconds ago.

'All done?' he asked, still keeping his distance, but the way his eyes dipped below her face before coming back up sent a shiver through her.

'Nothing to report here. You?' She knew he was about to tell her something, and whatever that was had him in a mood similar to a week ago. The air between them had crackled back then, too.

'We're stuck here until the storm subsides. They think it won't be longer than a few hours, but given that we worked throughout the night, they gave us a room.'

Larissa got off her chair, turning her head to look at the window. The pane was near black, the only interruption an occasional snow flurry pressing against the window as if trying to find a way inside. When the meaning of his words registered, she spun towards him. 'Wait, *room*, singular?'

His laugh was low and luxurious, skating over her skin like a warm caress. 'Space is tight here, so they don't have much when it comes to emergency housing.'

He pointedly looked around the room they had commandeered to do their physical exams. Someone had brought in a cot that she'd used as an exam table while ignoring the tables and rows of computers and other machines that she couldn't decipher. Whatever work usually went on in this room had to be paused for the research centre's annual health examination.

Larissa sighed, unwilling to give in to the heat pooling in the pit of her stomach just yet. They still needed to have that conversation. She wanted to know the things about him that he now knew about her, wanted to complete the picture of Erik that was becoming clearer by the day. But working through the night when she hadn't expected it had left her exhausted and struggling to think straight. Maybe a few hours of sleep would do her well, and then they could have that conversation on the way back.

And then...then they were free to act on the tension crackling between them.

'All right, lead the way,' she said, following on his heels as he ushered her down a corridor until they reached a non descript door among many non descript doors. Everything looked so much the same that she didn't quite know how he had the required certainty to push *this* exact door open.

But he did, and then he stepped back, letting her walk in first. A double bed stood against the wall, light grey sheets on the mattress, light gray cover on the duvet. Also singular, as Larissa noted. So they were either going to take turns sleeping, or—

Larissa turned around to face Erik, who had just closed the door. His hand still hovered on the door handle. She watched as his fingers slipped lower and tightened around the lock. The bolt slipped into place with a soft click, and somehow that sound was enough to release the tight grip Larissa had kept on her desire for Erik.

She surged towards him, and when he met her halfway, she realised he'd done the same. Fires erupted underneath her skin, sending heat coursing through her from head to toe.

His hand slipped over her back, his fingers dancing down her spine until he reached the hem of her shirt. She gasped into his mouth when his hand slid beneath the fabric and splayed over her ribs.

Then Erik tore his mouth from her, leaving her bereft of the sensation for a second before he pressed it against her neck. His beard scratched over her sensitive flesh, drawing another gasp that sounded more like a hiccup from her. Men were nothing new to her, but she'd forgotten what facial hair felt like. If her neck was already this sensitised after a brush of his lips, then what would happen to her once he—

'I'm so glad you joined me here,' he said as he trailed his tongue down her collarbone. His breath swept over her, sending shivers down her spine as she arched into his touch.

'You mean you're really glad I'm so bossy and pushed my way into this,' she replied, a huff between each other word.

Erik's chuckle skittered over her skin, finding the sensitive spots and burrowing inside her. He tugged at her shirt, and she gave him the space he needed to pull it over her head. Before he could

LUANA DAROSA 161

gather her back into his arms, she placed her hands on his chest and began to unbutton his shirt.

She let out a shaky sigh when she folded the fabric back over his shoulders, revealing the expanse of his torso. Larissa normally leaned more towards women, but this was... 'Oh my God.'

When Erik laughed again, she realised she had said it out loud. 'It was absolute torture to get through this week,' he huffed into her ear, his lips grazing the shell and sending another shockwave through her.

His hands now trailed her exposed flesh, finding the clasp of her bra and opening it again in a mirror of the last time. Only this time, there would be no interruptions.

Not willing to wait even a second longer, Larissa's hands got to work on the button of his trousers, pushing them down just as he pulled her bra down her arms, then made short work of removing her jeans. With both of them standing in front of each other in their underwear, Larissa let her eyes wander down his body—and felt him do the same.

Tight muscles rippled underneath pale skin as Erik breathed in and out, his hand flexing as if not touching her cost him whatever self-restraint remained within him. She planned on shattering that control.

Reaching out between them, Larissa trailed her hand from his chest down over his abs, her fingers tangling with the fine hair that led from his navel downwards and vanished past the waistband of his underwear.

She paused there, her breath growing heavy and her heart pounding in her throat. This was not the moment to retreat, to overthink it. They had their agreement, and Larissa would make sure he would say his part when they were done here. What else were they to do during a snowstorm? Plenty of time to give in to this thing building between them and see where the path led her.

'Well, we're here now.' She closed the gap between them and pressed the heel of her palm against his length. Erik's groan was low, his eyes fluttering closed for a second, and she felt the sensation race down her own spine. Her thighs clenched at the sound, and she knew when he touched her, he'd find her ready.

He huffed out another breath when she pushed down again, her fingers grazing over him, still wrapped in the fabric of his underwear. His hands shot up her body, burying themselves in her hair and pulling her head back. Then his mouth crashed down on her again, his kiss filled with the promise of passion.

'Get on the bed,' he said, voice low and gravelly—leaving her no room to argue. Not that she wanted to argue. The bed was exactly where she wanted to be.

'I see you're trying on the bossy pants now,' she couldn't help but say, even as she complied and sat down at the edge of the bed.

She watched with a predator's eye as Erik bent down, picking up his trousers and sticking his hand into a pocket. He pulled out a square of foil. Larissa's eyes widened.

'How could you have possibly brought condoms when you didn't even know I would be inviting myself on this field trip?' Her eyes travelled down his body as she said that, following his hands as he pushed down his underwear—exposing himself to her.

Her mouth went dry, and swallowing became a lot harder. Her heart was beating in her throat as Erik stepped out of the clothes discarded on the floor, ripping the foil open and then rolling on the condom.

'Whenever I come up here, I pack things they need. Prescriptions, first aid materials, books, board games.' He kept listing things as he came closer and stopped right in front of her. Towering over her. His gaze was ablaze as he raked it over her, his breath coming out heavy and uneven.

Then it dawned on her what he was saying. 'You stole the condoms meant for the researchers?'

Erik chuckled. 'I stole *one* condom. And I don't think it's stealing when the hospital purchased them.'

His hand came down on her naked thigh. Larissa made to move back to give him space, but his grip tightened as he shook his head. Then he knelt down in front of her, his body broad enough to push her thighs open. Skating up her legs, his hands reached the waistband of her underwear. And then he stopped. His fingers curling around the band, Erik looked up at her. Searching her face for an answer.

Permission.

Just when Larissa had thought she couldn't get any more turned on, he went and did this. Her heart leapt into her throat as she nodded. Then his warm breath grazed her sensitive flesh as he pulled down her underwear.

The roughness of his beard against her legs drew a gasp from her lips as he pressed his mouth along her inner thigh, kissing up towards her in a deliciously slow motion. Right towards the ache that had been building for him for far too long. An ache she'd tried to ignore, tried to explain away the best she could. Of course she was horny. Who wouldn't be on an island that was mostly ice and polar bears? Especially when the one hot guy on the aforementioned island worked in close quarters with her. That didn't mean any feelings were involved. They'd been clear about that. This was just an additional pastime for them to pursue—like reading books or playing board games.

'I've been thinking about this for so long,' Erik whispered as his lips trailed upward some more. His breath swept over her exposed sex, and the thought that he was breathing her in had her shivering. That he had fantasised about this moment just as much as she had.

'Please.' The word came out as a strangled noise that she didn't recognise as her own voice. *Please let me find out if it's as good as I imagined.* That was the meaning she was putting in one word, hoping he would pick up on it.

His fingers tightened around her thighs as he caressed her, and Larissa was about to make another attempt at speech when his breath hit her in that spot—right before his tongue did.

Her head lolled back as sensation exploded through her, a pent-up release already gathering at her spine. If she had found his fingers skillful, then his mouth was… There were no words for what his mouth was. Not as his fingers joined it, pushing into her and finding all the right spots. As if Erik had found a map of her body and studied it in preparation for this moment.

Larissa's breaths turned into pants, her skin growing more sensitive as she got closer to that cliff. The fresh linens rubbed against her skin as she bowed into his touch, arching off the bed entirely when the sensation became almost too much to withstand. But Erik was relentless in his willingness to pleasure her, his arm wrapped tightly around her hips and pinning her down as he licked and sucked and kissed her towards that iridescent veil gathering around her vision.

He didn't let up, not as she shuddered, feeling the pressure building at the base of her spine, her entire focus on the places where his body touched hers, and then—

Stars exploded behind her closed eyelids as release rushed through her, a loud sob tearing from her throat.

Her mind in pieces, Larissa lay there, catching her breath. A small sigh left her when Erik retreated—a strange emptiness rushing into the space where he'd just been—but then he reappeared on top of her as he got into the bed, pulling her limp body with him.

Her heart skipped a beat when he looked down at her, not with the blazing fire she'd seen in his eyes as they'd stripped down, but with an unexpected tenderness. As if he'd hidden it beneath the layers of need. But now, as he came to draw her into another kiss, this part of him slipped out.

'Erik, you—' He pressed his mouth against her again, his tongue slipping between her lips, and she thought that the taste alone would shatter her all over again.

'That's another way I know how to pleasure you now,' he said, and a shiver clawed down her spine when his body settled between her legs—his length pressing against her with a delicious pressure.

He looked down at her with nothing but tenderness and affection in his eyes as he asked, 'Are you ready to find out still another way?'

A shiver raked through her as their hips pressed together. Larissa nodded, and then her head lolled back again as Erik filled her.

Feeling Larissa all around him was a revelation Erik hadn't been prepared for by any measure. Another person couldn't possibly feel this *right*—this meant to be—in his own body. Need had driven him to this point, had taken him all the way to the brink with Larissa, and a shudder had raked through his own body as he watched her lose herself in his pleasure—again.

But this—there was something entirely different to this. She reacted as he moved in her, adjusting to his size, to his touch, guiding him where to go and how to touch. Always with a gentle kindness and a burning desire shining in her eyes.

The second Larissa fluttered around him, the pressure at the base of his spine intensified, signalling his own release. Erik thrust harder, picking up the tempo as her gasps of pleasure underneath him grew louder and the tension within them grew tighter.

He knew she was close. Knew it because he could feel it, and he was ready to go with her— dive over that cliff again. Because he knew there could be nothing as exquisite as their connection right at this moment. There was no way this could ever be replicated in any form, and he would hang on to it as long as he dared. As long as she'd let him.

'Larissa…' He breathed out her name as the pressure within him sharpened, his head coming down next to hers. Her breath skated over him, each pant and moan a warm blast over his sweat-covered skin.

'Don't slow down. This is—' Erik swallowed the rest of her words as he pressed his mouth against hers, drawing her into a kiss passionate enough to break him. His hands intertwined with hers, pinning her arms above her head as he thrust one more time, relishing the fluttering around him as release barrelled through him.

This wasn't supposed to be a mind-altering experience. They'd made it clear that whatever happened between them would never be more than a casual fling designed to end the moment Larissa stepped back on a plane—into her old life. But as her hands gripped him tighter and he slid off her to pull her into his arms, a quiet part of him wasn't entirely sure how he could let her go even if he knew he couldn't have her.

'Continue your story,' Larissa mumbled, her lips grazing over the back of his hand as she spoke.

Outside of crawling under the duvet, they hadn't moved much. Still naked, Erik had pulled her back flush against his front, and it was ridiculous how perfectly she fit him. Like some higher being had moulded her to sit right here against his body.

'My story?' His fingers drifted up and down her side, exploring every hill and valley of her and making a map of all her reactions to his touch.

'We said we're going into this with full honesty. To understand what happened so we don't fall into the same traps again.' She somehow scooted closer, her butt pressing against him enough that his manhood stirred again. There was no way he would ever have his fill of her.

'Right...' Working through all of his patients had been a new form of torture for him. Normally, he enjoyed getting out of Longyearbyen for a few hours and chatting with the researchers at this outpost. But after the conversation they'd had on the drive here, all he could think about was their discussion and what they'd agreed on, what he'd learned about Larissa.

The burn of indignity had been a constant companion to him throughout the consultations, and even now he couldn't wrap his head around why anyone would ever desire to change Larissa. How they could look at her and not see all the generosity and kindness and sweetness within her. He hadn't know her for long, and a growing part of him regretted that he wouldn't get the chance to know her better. Right next to him was a woman who, on her first day, had agreed to walk a sick patient's dog because she knew he couldn't. She knew nothing about Martin or his circumstances, yet she hadn't hesitated to do what was right to aid someone in his community—*her* community for as long as she remained.

To think someone had told her this wasn't enough was unfathomable. What terrified him about this entire thing was how he really wanted her to know him, too. Know how much he cared about his community and that by giving them as much of her as she had, she had found a way to touch his heart without realising it.

He took a deep breath and let it out slowly, thinking about where he'd left things off. 'My parents were thrilled to meet Astrid. Especially when she showed interest in the hotel. They never saw me much, and so for them, it was easy to assume I was some lonely hermit.'

Thinking back to the moment brought a dull pain with it, all wrapped up in his own naive outlook back then. 'I thought it was a sign. I liked her, could see myself growing to love her, and she seemed invested in Svalbard. I never thought I'd find someone who felt that way, which has always been the thing to stop me from getting close to anyone.'

Underneath his hand, Larissa shifted onto her back. Then she looked up at him, eyes alert but soft. 'So your parents seemed to value you more just because you were conforming with their idea of a happy life? That's a lot of pressure to put on someone.'

Erik snatched up her hand, pressing it against his mouth in a gentle kiss as her words kicked something loose inside him. The realisation that someone out there actually understood him.

Her.

She was right here, extracting the core of his complicated feelings in two sentences.

'With my parents as enthusiastic about her as they were, my mother soon slipped me the family heirloom engagement ring, and I just thought— this was another sign. Everything fit. My parents were happy for her to work at the hotel and to see me matched up, and I could serve the community in a way authentic to me—to who I am. We got engaged, and she moved into my cottage outside the village, and then…' His voice trailed off as the memories caught up with him.

Beside him, Larissa shifted, her hand coming down on his chest, gently pressing against his sternum. Her fingers curled into his hair there, the soft tugging reminding him she was here not to interrogate him but to hold space.

'Then she got bored. There's only so much that ever happens in Svalbard. I mean, you know the reality of what life is like here, and you're about to complete your first month here. It *is* boring if you lack an appreciation for the village and its people.' His greatest fear and the reason he'd never indulged in any serious relationship had come true in his life. He'd wanted to be wrong, wanted to be exposed as the cynic his family believed him to be. Astrid was meant to be that person who showed him he could have it all and still show up for his community the way he needed to.

His hand came up to where Larissa was stroking his skin, his fingers curling around hers. 'She wanted me to leave. Said that settling down in Svalbard had been a mistake, but that *I* wasn't. That I was the only right thing in her life, and that…' His voice faltered as he remembered that evening. The feeling of being torn in two direc-

tions at the same time still lingering in his soul.
'That if I loved her, I would consider moving
away with her.'

Just like that, she'd put him in front of the
choice he had never wanted to make. She had
believed so deeply that he would choose her, even
though he'd always been honest with her that if it
somehow came to that, he wouldn't—*couldn't*—
choose her. Because it wasn't who he was.

A rush of air leaving her nose was the only
noise Larissa made while he spoke, her eyes fixed
on where their fingers interlocked.

There it was. The truth that had only pushed
him further to dedicate himself to work. Now
Larissa knew to be wary of him when it came to
attachment. Because whoever wanted to be with
him needed to accept that his life—his heart—
belonged in Svalbard, and there was nothing that
would ever change that. This was his home, even
if it hurt sometimes.

Eventually, Larissa stirred. She tilted her head
upwards to look at him, and the way her eyes
brightened in the dim light of the bedside lamp
had the air rushing out of his lungs.

'Do you regret choosing the way you did?' she
asked, getting to the heart of his entire story in a
very Larissa way.

There was no hesitation as he shook his head.
'Not once. I have my regrets about how things

unfolded—the paths I allowed myself to be led down. But I won't ever regret choosing my people.'

He burned to know what she thought, but her expression remained veiled, not letting him see beyond the surface. He wasn't sure *why* he wanted to know. There was no real opinion to be had. He'd told her his story.

'Thank you for telling me. Now that I know, I promise I will slink quietly back to England when my time is up without making any great declarations.' She looked up at him, and her smirk sent a shiver trickling down his spine. 'I promise I won't fall in love with you.'

His stomach bottomed out as he heard the words he wanted to hear. A wave of ice sloshed through his veins, reaching out to his limbs until his entire body was cold. His grip around Larissa tightened, pulling her closer into his body as if he could borrow her warmth.

'Good,' he whispered into her hair, the scent of her so intoxicating, he closed his eyes to ground himself. 'I promise I won't, either.'

CHAPTER NINE

THE EVER-DIM LIGHT of the hotel's common room hummed with the activity of a few scattered groups of people. Larissa paid them no mind as she stretched her legs out in front of her.

This was what cats had to feel like. They got to lounge around furniture all day and receive food as if magic conjured it up. Larissa didn't know because she'd never actually had a cat—or any other pet. With the time she spent at work in the past, she thought another human was too hard to accommodate, let alone an animal that couldn't even communicate with her in words. Granted, a lot of humans didn't do that, either, though that was mostly because of a lack of willingness.

Somehow she and Erik had figured out how to be honest with each other without descending into the chaos that was romantic feelings. Learning more about him, about the things he'd been through with his ex-fiancée, had unlocked a piece of the Erik puzzle that she'd been staring at since the moment she'd met him without understanding how to get closer to him.

'You need anything else, just let me know,' Hilde said as she set down the steaming cup next to Larissa on a small side table to the right of the armchair Larissa had claimed for herself.

'Thank you.' She smiled at the older woman and took a sip of the hot chocolate, her eyes fluttering shut as the taste flooded her mouth. It was absolutely divine and led Larissa to question her life choices not for the first time since she'd arrived here. Why had she and Ally put up with the sewage water that they served at Heaton Perk for so long when tastes like *this* existed?

Digging out her phone, Larissa took the mug into her hand and balanced it on her knee, right next to the book in her lap, and took a picture. Then she sent it to Ally without a caption. Her friend probably wouldn't see the picture until tomorrow. They'd agreed to read the same book over their time away, though the more involved Larissa got with Erik, the less time there was for reading. Surely Ally wouldn't mind…

Fairy lights on the inside had joined the ones on the outside of the house and wound their way across the beams on the ceiling. They blinked, the colour fading from white to pink to red. Vases with roses stood on the scattered tables. Coming down earlier, Larissa had spotted a poster announcing the activities for the residents of the Aurora Hotel for Valentine's Day.

Her stomach lurched at the thought. The day was coming up, and she had no plans. Of course she didn't, because she wasn't in a relationship. It would be weird if she spent the day with Erik, wouldn't it?

'Are you enjoying yourself?' The familiar female voice had her glancing up and into a face that looked so much like Erik's, Larissa lost her train of thought for a moment.

'Um… yes,' she said as Anna slid into the armchair across from her, smiling big enough to show a neat row of white teeth. 'I have the day off today. Well, not really. I'm on call, so I can't go far from the hospital. Not that I could do that even if I wasn't on call. But I thought I'd come down here and find something to occupy my time while watching the pager.'

She lifted the book from her lap, showing Anna the title. The woman's smile grew even wider. '*A Court of Thorns and Roses*? Nice choice.'

'Did you read it?'

Anna nodded, a spark illuminating her eyes. 'Oh yeah, any of the new books here are mine. My father contributed all the cold war novels. I don't know how he can read them. It's always the same. Spy man on some spy mission to save the spy world from the brink of spy…something.'

'Spy something?' Larissa asked, barely containing her laughter.

'Ah, you know. Man saves the world. Boring.' She waved her hand in front of her, and Larissa couldn't help it—she instantly took a liking to Anna. Why hadn't she interacted much with the woman before?

Maybe because she looked so much like her brother, who Larissa had become so wrapped up in that she didn't really have the capacity for anyone else. No, that wasn't true. She was *not* wrapped up in Erik at all. Maybe in his sheets, but that was the maximum wrapping she would do to him.

It didn't matter if he might have a charming sister, and Larissa *definitely* didn't wonder how she figured into the entire difficult relationship dynamic he'd shared with her. Because they hadn't opened up to each other to get closer to one another. No, the sole purpose of the emotional striptease they'd gone through was purely research—so they could avoid making this something that it wasn't.

'Well, this is definitely *not* man saves the world.' Larissa wasn't sure what exactly this was, but she'd seen the title talked about often enough on TikTok that she and Ally had picked this one to tandem read.

Anna leaned across the space, and Larissa

tilted the book towards her when prompted, so she could look at the page number. Her eyes widened. 'Ah, it's about to start,' she said with a conspiratorial twinkle before leaning back. 'It's nice to see you down here unwinding. Hope my brother isn't riding you too hard at the hospital.'

Larissa coughed, almost spitting hot chocolate all over the book. Setting the mug down on the side table, she tapped her hand against her sternum. 'Sorry, I, um, forgot which way liquids go. Turns out the oesophagus and not the windpipe,' she said, hoping she'd covered up what had *actually* made her cough.

'Ah, yes. I hear that happens a lot,' Anna replied, and the small smile spreading over her lips had Larissa wondering if Erik had told his sister anything.

'He usually lets me have the weekends off. Though today I'm on call until Erik is back, which should be any minute.' She lifted a pager covered in rhinestones from the side table, showing it off. 'Since I have to be dressed for any emergencies, I thought I might as well sit by the fire.'

'Good choice.' Anna eyed the pager, then looked back at her. 'Please tell me you glued these rhinestones on to piss my brother off.'

Larissa chuckled. 'Ingrid and I did it yesterday after two appointments were cancelled.' She turned the pager around in her hand. 'I think he'll love it.'

Anna nodded, amusement dancing in her eyes. 'Yes, if my brother loves anything, it's *definitely* change. Never met someone who dealt with it better.'

Putting the pager back down, she straightened in her chair, trying not to be too obvious as she eyed the other woman. Even though they looked so much like each other, the auras around Erik and Anna were so different. Like they were polar opposites. She remembered when Erik had picked her up for her first day. He'd spoken to his sister, but they hadn't exchanged more than a few words. Back then, Larissa hadn't even thought of paying it any kind of attention. Neither of them had been more than strangers to her.

But now… Now she felt like she knew who Erik was. Not someone who wore his heart on his sleeve, but someone who valued the ties to his community and the people around him. Valued them so much that he was willing to give up large pieces of himself just to ensure he was keeping his people safe. That his fiancée had asked him to give it all up was…

'How could anyone ever get bored with this?' Larissa asked out loud, and Anna raised her eyebrows.

'Why do you ask…' Her voice trailed off, the

amused sparkle in her eyes disappearing as she tilted her head to the side.

Oh no… Had that question revealed too much about what Erik had told her? 'What I mean is that—'

A figure appearing behind Anna's chair caught their attention, and Larissa swallowed a relieved sigh. Erik towered over them, brushing the snowflakes out of his hair. The twinkling lights wreathed him in a soft pink glow as a smile spread across his lips, and the paper hearts hanging from the ceiling looked like they were sprouting from his head. His expression changed from neutral to inquisitive as his gaze bounced between Larissa and his sister.

'What are you doing here?' Anna asked, glancing up at him.

A wave of awareness rushed over Larissa, and to keep herself busy, she reached for her mug, half hiding her face behind it. What *was* he doing here? She knew he'd arrive today, but had totally not been looking at her phone every few minutes to see if a message from him had appeared. That would be weird, and Larissa was definitely *not* weird. Nope.

'I just got back from a meeting in Norway. Thought I'd stop by,' he said with a casual shrug, then looked around before grabbing a nearby chair and pulling it towards them. When he peeled his jacket off, Anna sat up straighter.

'Blir du? Her?' Larissa blinked at the woman as she switched to Norwegian.

Erik sat down, draping one leg over the other and looking at his younger sister with a raised eyebrow. 'Yes,' he answered, and Larissa wasn't sure what underpinned his voice. Was he annoyed at the question? What had she asked?

Before Larissa could inquire, he added, 'That's not a problem, is it?'

Anna quickly shook her head. 'Not a problem at all,' she said, following his lead and sticking to English.

Larissa didn't have any siblings, so the dynamic between them had always seemed like a strange concept to her. Her friends had often complained about their brothers and sisters growing up, but her parents had decided one was enough. These days she was almost certain they had decided that even one was too much, and that had been the whole reason they'd been at each other's throats so much. Their relationship was so overwhelming that they didn't have space for something additional to it—including their own daughter.

But she knew enough about interpersonal relationships to sense something odd about the siblings' exchange. Like Anna either didn't want him here or…was she surprised? Erik had said that he didn't come to visit often. That didn't mean never. She'd seen him here before, had she not? The night she'd arrived, he came here to greet her. Maybe he never lingered around for long?

'How was the trip to Norway?' she asked when silence spread between them, the vibe more awkward than she was used to.

'Good. Needed to talk to some people at the health ministry to discuss funding and research for next year,' he said as he relaxed into the chair, his shoulders slowly drooping. From where Anna sat in her armchair, she was still studying her brother, though her expression didn't let Larissa guess what she might be thinking.

'Research?' Larissa asked. 'Like medical research?'

But Erik shook his head. 'Research like the facility we visited last week. I need to know how many people are sent to Svalbard for long-term research purposes so I can account for their medical needs,' he said, and Larissa nodded. 'Thanks for taking over my on-call shift.'

Larissa waved her hand in front of her dismissively. 'Oh, don't worry about it. I can't believe that all this time you were the one fielding *all* the on-call emergencies.'

'I can believe it. Erik has been running the

off-hours medical support since they put him in charge of the hospital,' Anna muttered, earning herself a glare from her brother.

'Wait, really?' Larissa's eyes widened when the information sank in. 'You are the only doctor who is ever on call? *Ever?*'

Erik only shrugged, like this wasn't a big deal. She'd thought that he just didn't want her to do any on-call things since it might require her to leave the village. She opened her mouth to protest and point out that this might be really dangerous. What if he got a call late at night after a long day at the hospital? What if he was sleep-deprived?

But before she could say anything, he cut in, 'I assume there was no need for anything?'

'There were no calls outside of minor things that the nurse on shift could take care of,' Larissa said, picking up the now *very* sparkly pager.

Erik stared at it, slowly blinking a few times. 'What on earth is that?'

The reaction was exactly what Larissa had hoped for, and she couldn't fight the grin spreading over her face. Even Anna was trying—and failing—to contain her laughter as Erik pinned the object in her hand with his glare.

'Oh, the rhinestones? Yeah, they are an additional safety measure,' she said, taking a deep breath to swallow her amusement when his eyes narrowed.

'Safety measure?' he repeated, each word coming out after a beat of contemplation as if she was speaking a different language.

'That's right. If you dropped the pager in the snow, it was hard to find with a torch because it was matte. Now that it glitters, it's very easy to find when hit by a light source.' She twisted the pager in her hand, and the light of the fire caught in the rhinestones. A kaleidoscope of colourful dots of light bounced around the common room as she rotated her hand.

'You're messing with—' Erik stopped midsentence when the pager gave off a shrill sound, its vibrations shaking her hand.

Flipping it around, she looked at the message crawling across the screen. Her heart skipped a beat when it got to the end and looped around once more.

Emergency: Animal attack reported 2 km east of Longyearbyen near Glacier Point. Two victims, one unconscious. Incident reported by victim. Bear sighted in the area. Immediate medical assistance required. Evac helicopter notified.

She handed the pager to Erik, who only glanced at it for a second before jumping to his feet. Not even two minutes later, they sped away on his snowmobile towards Glacier Point.

The temptation to leave Larissa behind burned at the back of his neck as they approached Glacier

Point. An active animal attack was a rare emergency to deal with, as most people understood the dangers of leaving Longyearbyen. Still, some believed the law that they had to be armed at any time to be a mere suggestion. Those people were almost always tourists with more bravery than brains to go around. No one actually living here would ever forget that they were mere guests on the island and that the polar bears and other wildlife were the true inhabitants of Svalbard.

The snowmobile's high beams revealed a large area of the snowfield, and he slowed down as they looked. The last thing they needed was to run head first into an already agitated polar bear. Erik would hate to have to use his rifle, but he knew he wouldn't hesitate for even a second. Her safety was the most important thing here.

Our safety, he corrected himself as he came to a halt and the arms clinging to him loosened. This was not about Larissa; it couldn't be. They had agreed what their fling would be like, and nothing would ever change his mind about needing to be here in Svalbard.

He knew that in his head, yet his chest still tightened thinking about letting her go—about putting her in dangerous situations such as this one. Would he have had similar qualms with someone else accompanying him for this incident?

Erik pushed the thought away, not liking the

answer that awaited him in the depths of his heart.

'Take the torch and shine it around. See if you can find any tracks.' Larissa nodded and half turned before he snatched her wrist, closing his hand around it. 'Do not move even a step in any direction without me, okay?'

Larissa's eyes widened, her breath gathering in a big cloud in front of her, and the intensity of his voice took Erik aback. Clearly she had been taken aback, too. 'You're unarmed,' he added to soften his words.

'Okay,' she breathed out, underlining it with a nod, and then Erik let go of her arm—only for instant regret to flood him all over again. It was way too dangerous out here for her. What would he do if...

Again, he swatted the thoughts away. They were leading him down a path he couldn't walk. One where he couldn't think straight because he was too worried, too focused on the wrong thing.

'I think I see some footprints over there,' Larissa said beside him, pointing the powerful beam of her heavy-duty torch at a patch of snow further away.

Erik unslung the rifle from his back, one hand tightening around the stock while the other came up around the trigger, keeping his finger near the trigger guard with the barrel facing downward.

'Keep shining the light there and follow behind me,' he said, monitoring her as they walked towards the disturbance in the snow.

'Two sets of footprints,' he said as they stopped in front of them, and Larissa followed their trail with the light when—

'There they are!' She pointed with her free hand at a dark figure huddled over another one. After exchanging a quick glance, Erik nodded at her, and together they hurried over.

Larissa kneeled down beside the patient. Erik pulled the headlamp out of his jacket pocket, put it on and pushed the switch before turning in a circle. There was no trace of a bear, but there were some markings in the distance that could be footprints—or paw prints.

'What is your name?' Larissa addressed the person kneeling next to her, who seemed unharmed at first glance.

'Kaiden,' the man replied, his face almost as white as the surrounding snow. The woman's head was in his lap, her eyes pinched shut and her breath coming out in shallow pants.

'I'm Larissa, and this is Erik. We're doctors from the hospital. What happened here?'

Erik's eyes flicked around, monitoring their surroundings as Kaiden spoke.

'We went out with our tour guide last week, and Ashley, s-she wanted to take some more pictures before we leave tomorrow. We didn't mean to go far, just a few steps to catch some undisturbed snow, but then we got lost in the dark.' A low whimper drew Erik's attention downwards to the patient. The film of sweat on her scrunched-up brow was concerning.

Larissa nodded, working on identifying the patient's injuries.

'The distress call mentioned a potential animal attack,' Larissa said, following his line of thought unprompted. Something soft unfurled inside his chest, but he pushed it away. There would be plenty of time to figure *that* out later.

'We were just wandering around when our light went out. When we heard crunching in the snow and realised it was a bear, we ran, but she slipped, and she must have hurt her leg.' Kaiden kept his hands on her head as he spoke, looking down at her with the worry on his face growing.

Larissa kept her eyes on him, nodding him along his tale. When he'd finished, she examined the patient, her hands slowly working downwards with enough pressure to feel through the layers of clothing.

He watched as she paused and then shifted the patient's legs apart. The second she moved one leg a millimetre to the side, Ashley gasped before groaning into the quiet.

'Something wrong with her leg?' Erik asked, stepping closer to Larissa to give her more light.

Ashley groaned again when Larissa pushed her hands underneath the leg, carefully lifting it a finger-width off the ground and checking below. 'Potentially a break. We'd have to take off her clothes to inspect it. But I don't see any blood on the snow.'

Erik looked up at Ashley, whose stuttering breath showed her level of pain. A sprain wouldn't take someone out in such a way. A break was more likely.

Larissa gave Kaiden a reassuring smile before getting onto her feet and stepping closer to Erik. A flash of pride pulsed through him when her eyes darted around their environment the same way his had. She was behaving like a local.

'I can't tell the severity of the break like that,' she said as she pulled him a few steps away and out of earshot of Kaiden. 'It might still be an open fracture with how much pain she's in and how she reacts to being moved. Do we strip her even in these temperatures?'

Erik shook his head. 'Sometimes we do, but I'm comfortable being more conservative here. The medevac is already en route. Once she's in there, we can stabilise the break with the help of the evacuation team. It'll be warmer there.'

'But what if she is bleeding under the clothes and we just can't see it?'

Erik looked towards the patient, considering their options. They could wait for the helicopter. That would keep Ashley warm, though if she had a wound that needed attention, she could risk losing a lot of blood. Or they could cut off as much of her clothes as necessary for a proper examination and stabilise whatever damage they found. He had a few heat packs along with some blankets at the bottom of his backpack, but the risk of hypothermia would be so much higher than it already was.

'What did you feel?' he asked, hoping this would give him a clue on which way to lean. But Larissa only shook her head.

'Nothing that would lead me to believe there was a compound fracture. But I've never examined anyone wearing these gloves.' She held up her hands, showing off her heavy insulated gloves. 'Have you?'

He paused for a second before he nodded. Erik knew what she was going to suggest next, and it had been the thing he'd hoped to avoid.

'You examine her, then,' she said, and her brow creased when he didn't move.

'There might still be a polar bear around us.'

'I'll stay right beside you. Keep an eye out so that we don't get surprised. You know it won't charge at us out of nowhere.' Chances were unlikely that a polar bear would attack such a large group, but Erik had seen and heard weirder things happen. Especially if they were near its territory.

He wouldn't hesitate to inspect the patient if it was just him. If danger arose, he could get a shot out before it might be too late. But he had Larissa to worry about, and if she…

Erik squeezed his eyes shut. This was exactly the reason he shouldn't see people. Instead of thinking about the right thing to do for his patient, he was distracted, too worried about Larissa being in harm's way to act as he usually would.

'Okay, let me have a look,' he said, even though everything inside him protested against turning his back and lowering his weapon.

Before he could lose his nerve, he walked back towards the patient and took a knee while making sure the rifle stayed right by his side.

'We are evaluating our best options. The helicopter is already on the way to get you out of here, but we're not sure how to secure Ashley for the transport,' he said to Kaiden as he wrapped his hands around her leg and applied enough pressure that he could get some idea of what lay beneath her clothes.

'Ashley—she was in a lot of pain when she fell, but she grew quieter and… We need to get her out of here.' The edge of panic rang in Kaiden's voice, one Erik felt slicing through his chest. Suddenly, he knew such fear all too well.

'There are two things that might cause that. She might have broken her leg during her fall, which seems likely with how sensitive she is in that area. If it is a compound fracture, she might be bleeding.' Kaiden's eyes went wide. 'Or it might be hypothermia from lying motionless on the cold ground for a prolonged time. Either way—'

He paused when a faint sound caught his attention. 'I can hear the rescue helicopter.' Erik slid his hand further down, slowing when Ashley twitched with a painful groan. It was still hard to tell, but… 'I don't think it's a compound fracture. With the helicopter nearby, I say we'll wait for them to arrive. We will have an easier time stabilising her leg inside the helicopter.'

Kaiden nodded, and Erik slung his pack off his back, opening the top and digging through the supplies they had brought until he found the blankets and heat packs. 'Let's get her as warm as possible until they arrive, so when we—'

'Erik.' Larissa's voice was quiet, but the warning etched into his name was enough to freeze the blood in his veins.

His head whipped around, looking in the direction she was facing—and spotted the dark shadow moving towards them. All thoughts emptied out of his brain.

All he could see was Larissa in the direct path of the animal, frozen into place. Around them the helicopter noises grew louder, and through the frantic beating of his heart, Erik forced himself to remain calm. This was no different from any encounters he'd had with the wildlife here. Nothing he didn't know intimately already, except if Larissa got hurt… if he lost—

'We need to shoot up the flare gun so the helicopter can find us. Chances are the noise and brightness will be enough to scare the bear away,' Erik said, forcing himself to focus solely on the things he could control. His reaction and attachment to Larissa clearly weren't two of those things.

'What do you want me to do?' she asked, her voice steadier than he would have expected.

'Take a few steps back. But stay upright and as large as you can be. Don't crouch, and no sudden movements.' Erik stuck his hand into his pack again, finding the flare gun almost at the top and yanking it out. Then he stood, stepping around the patient and walking towards Larissa, who took slow and steady paces backwards with her arms raised. She kept facing forward, each step a loud crunch in the snow that echoed across the empty snow field.

'A few more steps and you'll be in my reach,' Erik said, his voice so strained he wasn't sure who he was trying to reassure: her or himself?

In the distance, the shadowy bear ambled towards them, its eyes lighting up when Erik's lamp caught them at the right angle. Just two more steps and then—

Erik raised the hand holding the flare over his head while he stretched out the other one towards Larissa. As his fingertips connected with her back, he squeezed the trigger of the flare. A glaring red light shot upwards with a loud bang, and underneath his hand, he felt Larissa flinch at the sound. But so did the bear, fully illuminated for a few seconds as the flare raced up into the sky. It reared back from the sound, stirring up a cloud of snow as it ran away into the distance.

The pressure in his chest eased instantly as the animal ran off. Before he could even think about doing differently, he hauled Larissa into his arms, pressing her against him. All the stress and anxiety of the last few minutes went into that hug, into holding her close until his terrified mind knew she was safe.

'I'm okay, Erik,' she said near his ear, mirroring the thoughts in his head.

She was fine. Safe. Yet his arms wouldn't let go. Not until the roaring of the helicopter was right above them.

'Help is here,' she said, and he nodded as he finally stepped away from her, the fear of losing her still clinging to him in a cold sweat.

Larissa was okay, but he wasn't sure if he would be after this moment—after seeing how deeply her safety affected him. How could he let her go at the end of her assignment?

CHAPTER TEN

'IT'S VALENTINE'S DAY.' Ally's familiar voice filtered out of the phone's speaker, filling the room.

'It sure is,' Larissa replied, looking between her friend's face and the view beyond her window. Like she could ever forget it was Valentine's Day when the entire hotel was decorated with roses, paper hearts and blinking lights.

'Two weeks and then we're back in England.'

'That's exactly right.'

Silence stretched between them, which wasn't unusual for them. They were at a point in their friendship where they could spend hours with each other and only exchange a few words. But that had been when they were closely working with each other and witnessing every moment of each other's lives. Now they were several thousand kilometres away from one another, and there were more than enough things they needed to discuss. Only Larissa didn't want to mention any of them because they involved Erik.

And she had an inkling that Ally was rather quiet for the same reasons.

Ever since they'd returned from the research centre, they'd been sneaking around—exclusively at the hospital after the other staff had gone home. With his parents being far too interested in his love life, they couldn't come here, and he hadn't invited her to his place. Though she tried not to dwell on that.

They weren't a couple, so she couldn't expect anything of him.

'Do we do our usual thing? Order food and watch an entire season of *The Great British Bake Off*?'

Ally frowned. 'I don't know if I can stream it from here. Getting messages through to you is sometimes a struggle. Anyway, I thought you'd have other plans?'

They fell quiet again, and Larissa stared at her friend, her own frown deepening. She would have to bring it up, wouldn't she? The last thing she wanted was to dive deep into whatever was happening between her and Erik.

No, she needed a different topic. So she blurted out the only other thing she could think of that they hadn't talked about. 'I almost got eaten by a bear.'

'Wait, what?' Ally's eyebrows rose. 'Your confession is not about Thor? I thought that's why you're being depresso espresso on Valentine's Day.'

'What? No, I'm not in love with Erik.' Heat rushed up her neck and into her face as she uttered her denial, and she ignored the tightness around her chest at those words. Of course she wasn't in love with Erik. That wasn't possible. They had both agreed that anything above a friendship with certain benefits would be far too complicated to navigate.

'So why are you moping around on Valentine's Day? Why aren't you lighting up the town with your Nordic god impersonator?' Ally crossed her arms in front of her chest, pushing out her chin in a defiant challenge. Like Larissa telling the truth about her feelings was somehow an affront to her friend.

'Light up the town? You mean go to one of the three bars that I've been to several times already and have a beer before slinking back to the hospital?' She paused, worried how nice the thought sounded. Though instead of going back to the hotel, Larissa would prefer to go to Erik's cabin, where they could have some alone time. Outside of a few stolen—and perilous—moments at the hospital, they hadn't really spent the night together since they'd returned from their trip to the research outpost.

'You talk about him *every day*,' Ally insisted, poking further into feelings Larissa would rather remain unexplored.

'Yeah, so? I talk about you every day. Doesn't mean I'm in love with you. Is that what you're suggesting? That you would totally move to a little island for someone you happen to talk about every day so that you could be together, even though that would put us several time zones away? And who even has the time to remain friends? Certainly not you when you are slipping deep into that new relationship energy.'

Ally tilted her head far enough that her ear touched her shoulder as she looked at Larissa through the screen of her phone. 'I didn't suggest any of this,' she said, brows high on her forehead. 'I think there is a rather curious dose of projection happening. You think staying in Svalbard would break our friendship? Because I can tell you I have never heard something this ridiculous in my life.'

'What? No. There's no projecting going on. I'm talking about hypotheticals.'

'Larry…'

'What I said wouldn't ever be true, because he doesn't want to leave Svalbard, and I could never move here. My life is in Frome. With you.' Was this woman seriously trying to make this about *him*? Because that was ridiculous. Her feelings for Erik didn't run any deeper than their casual fling allowed. She couldn't let herself go there.

'I don't think you're being honest with yourself,' Ally said, her voice soft, yet her words stung anyway as they rang familiar in her mind. They'd had a similar conversation before everything with Rachel had gone up in flames. She'd been right about her not wanting to see the truth back then, too.

'Okay, so, even if I were into him—which I'm still disputing—he is clearly not that hot on me. I mean, I'm sitting here all by myself on Valentine's Day, and he knows I'm not doing anything. Or anyone.'

Ally opened her mouth to reply, but a knock from the door interrupted her. Larissa looked between her friend and the door before calling out, 'Who is it?'

'It's Erik,' a deep voice said. Even though the door muffled the sound, she knew from the high-pitched squeal coming from her phone that Ally had heard it.

'He came to get you for V-Day,' her friend whispered, eyes wide enough that Larissa could see her irises changing into an obnoxious heart shape like a cartoon character's.

'I promise you he didn't,' Larissa replied, though a small and traitorous part inside her wondered the same thing. 'I'll call you back in a bit.'

Larissa hit the disconnect button just as her friend's face transformed with shock, and then stood up, opening the door to the man she had apparently manifested here by denying the depth of their connection. He leaned against the doorframe with his signature subdued smile that grew brighter as he saw her.

'You keep on coming to see me at the hotel. Either I should feel very honoured or the nosiness of your family was overly dramatised,' she said, and then immediately regretted the words. How could she make light of something he'd told her in confidence? How would she feel if he made jokes about her dysfunctional family?

But Erik only huffed out a laugh as he righted himself. 'Their schedules are quite rigid. I know when I can sneak in without being seen,' he said, amusement lighting up his face.

'So I'm your secret?' Larissa tried her best to sound playful but didn't quite stick her landing. She winced when her words sounded far more needy than she meant to come across.

'In this scenario, *I'm* the secret,' he said, and then he took a step closer, putting himself squarely in her space.

Larissa had to look up to keep eye contact, though that didn't last all that long as Erik bent his head down to brush a kiss onto her lips.

'I just finished up at the hospital and wondered if you want to have dinner tonight?' he asked when their lips parted, though his face remained close to hers so that each of his breaths swept across her cheeks.

'Where do you want to go?' His scent enveloped her, making it so much harder to remember all the things she'd just assured Ally. They really shouldn't go on a date on Valentine's Day. That's what people who meant something to each other did.

'Let's pick up some things at the shop and go to my place. No chance of being overheard by certain people.' He angled his mouth over hers as he said that, dragging her into another kiss that had her knees trembling with the effort to keep her upright.

So this really was a date. Then she should definitely say no. This would be far from appropriate and only prove Ally's point that she was in a relationship-type situation when she knew she wasn't.

'Plus, I want to show you something tomorrow morning. I had hoped it would happen today but... well, let's say the stars didn't align,' he added, breathing another kiss onto her lips.

Show her something? That was enough to poke at her curiosity and gave her a reason to ignore the cautious voice in her head telling her that if she spent Valentine's Day at his house, she would slip far too deep into this thing between them to find her way out again.

'What are you making me?'

There was something just right about seeing Larissa surrounded by his things. She lay on a plush carpet in front of the fire burning in his small fireplace, staring into the flames as if in a trance. And right next to her lay Midnight, her snout wedged underneath Larissa's hand and begging for ear scratches that she was all too willing to give.

'She will be insufferable with me now when you're not around,' Erik said as he rounded the couch and got onto the floor next to her.

Larissa gave Midnight another rub before turning around so she was facing him. A lazy smile spread over her lips, and Erik couldn't help it. He reached out and traced her lips with his thumb before touching her cheek.

'I was really worried about you out there when we responded to the animal attack,' he said, his fingers tangling into the stray strands of hair on her face.

'I know, but you prepared me well for the situation, Erik. I was fine and in no more danger than any of the others.' He knew that was true, saw the logic in it himself. But despite all of that, the fear that had gripped him was of a different kind altogether. Primal. And an indicator of how far he had let things go between them. How his feelings had taken over any rational thinking.

Even now, all he could think about was how he wanted her around in his cottage because, according to his brain, she was the missing piece in his life. Two hours in here and the place already *felt* different. Apparently, he'd been waiting for something—someone—very specific to appear and make it all fit. He'd tried so hard to do that with Astrid, had bent and broken himself to glue things together and give the illusion of wholeness.

'I enjoy seeing this,' he said, even though he didn't know why—or where he was heading with the observation. At the very least, he knew that they'd promised to be truthful with each other. But whether what he was about to say was a truth that needed to be said, he wasn't sure.

'You like seeing what? Your spoiled dog stealing all of my warmth?' Larissa replied, chuckling.

'Yes, I like that you're in her space and she's perfectly happy with that. I like…seeing you in my cottage. You fit right in here.' Erik had no idea what he was trying to accomplish other than letting her know him—know this new feeling inside his chest, even though they would only share the thing between them for a short two weeks.

Her lips parted as his words sank in. The words

that sounded so much like a confession he was not ready to give. Would never be ready to give because their lives didn't align in such a way.

But lying down on the floor of his cottage and holding her close to him, he could no longer deny how she made his heart soar to new heights. How genuine terror had gripped him when he'd thought she was in danger and when he'd played out the thought of losing her so soon. That was a dark place he didn't want to return to.

Despite all of his best efforts to keep her away from the soft part inside his chest, Larissa had wiggled her way past his defences, and he was now at her mercy—in love with this woman he shouldn't want as much as he did.

'Erik, I… It's so beautiful here. When we came here to walk Martin's dog, I already wanted to know what it looks like in here.' She made a show of looking past him and around the small living room. 'It's much nicer than my hotel room—no offence to your birthright, of course,' she quickly added, and Erik laughed.

'No offence taken. They are cosy rooms but not really designed for full-time occupancy.' His hand drifted lower, grazing over her neck before slipping down her arm and relishing the goose pimples he left on her skin as his fingertips moved downwards. Then he said another thing he knew he should keep to himself, but something about her lying in his arms took him into places he promised himself he wouldn't go.

'Why don't you stay here? It'll be more comfortable for you, and I enjoy having you close.' To emphasise his point, he drew her closer and pressed a gentle kiss onto her lips.

This probably wasn't a good idea. His parents would notice that she hadn't been in her room for ages, and he would be the first suspect in her sudden disappearance. But he needed her close, regardless of what the rumours would be. This was ending in two weeks, and he would have every second of those.

Larissa hummed against his lips, a sound he'd grown to love. Like the pressure of his lips against hers was enough to send sparks of pleasure ricocheting through her—which was true for him, too. This connection was unlike anything he'd ever experienced. It made him wish that things were different. That he could be someone who left—or asked people to stay. But Erik was still Erik. Nothing had changed, so nothing *could* change between them.

Larissa huffed when they parted, her lips swollen and red from where his beard had rubbed against her face. The sight sent a flash of arousal racing down his spine, and he pushed himself closer to her.

Larissa gasped, shivering against his length

now pressed between them. 'Are you asking me to stay here with you? Move in here with you?'

Her breath grazed his face, her scent enveloping him, making it hard to keep his thoughts straight. The softness pressing against him drained all the blood from his upper body, and his desire for her left no room for anything else.

Move in? Yes, that would make the rest of their arrangement far easier. What had her confused about that?

'Yes, stay here with me. If that's what you want, too.' To underline his words, he flexed his hips so he pushed against her again, and Larissa's eyes fluttered shut for a moment.

That Larissa would spend more time here changed nothing between them. She still wanted to leave and rebuild her life in England while he remained rooted to Svalbard. They both agreed that there was no way for them to live a life together that wasn't temporary. But if a temporary life was the only thing he could get, he still wanted to make the best of it.

'Wake up, beautiful.' Erik's low voice enveloped her, and Larissa sank deeper into the warmth that surrounded her. This sleep had been the best in days—weeks even. There was no way she was going to pass up this time by waking up. No thanks.

The bed shook slightly, threatening to fully pull her out of her sleepy state, and then Erik's warm mouth pressed kisses on her bare shoulder and slowly travelled up her neck until he reached her ear. 'We need to get dressed. There's something I want to show you, remember?'

Larissa opened her eyes, but her lids were way too heavy, and gravity won this battle as she closed them again. Above her, Erik chuckled, his arms wrapping around her and pulling her into his solid front. Her body melded against his as if they'd been made for each other, her curves fitting perfectly into the dips and valleys that were Erik.

This moment was perfect, and she didn't want it to slip away.

'I promise you it's worth it. We can crawl straight into bed again afterwards. Unless someone pages with an emergency, I don't have any plans today.' His voice was low and soft and enveloped her with a different warmth. Her foggy mind reached out to his words, grasping at them, and with a sigh, she forced her eyes open again.

A warm light coming from an alarm clock on his bedside table lit up the small bedroom, and Larissa turned towards it. She squinted to make out the numbers on the display, and when the time of day clicked into place, she widened her eyes and sat up in bed.

'It's almost nine? How did I sleep so long?' Without the sun giving her any indication of when to get up, Larissa had developed the habit of getting up at six and starting her day by calling or texting Ally before heading over to the hospital. Even on the days she didn't need to go to work, her body now automatically woke up at the right time.

Erik sat up with her as he gave a shrug. 'My alarm clock lit up at six, but the light didn't seem to bother you.'

She glanced over at Erik, looking down at his exposed torso. On its own accord, her hand went up to smooth over the dark blond hair covering his chest. The coarse feeling sent a shiver down her spine and shook the last vestiges of sleep from her.

'Good morning,' he said as he bent over to brush a kiss over her lips. Larissa melted against him, soaking in the warmth of his body, and was all but ready to lose herself in his touch again when he grabbed her by the shoulders and pushed her away.

'If you don't get dressed now, we might miss it,' he said. Before she could reel him in again, he rolled out of bed and began collecting his clothes off the floor.

Bundled up in all the layers she usually put on for an excursion into the icy fields of Svalbard,

Larissa sat on a bench on Erik's porch. A soft cloud of steam rose from the insulated mug in her hands whenever she opened the lid to take a sip. Erik sat next to her, his arm casually draped around her shoulders and pulling her into his warm body.

She'd been wrong earlier. *This* moment was perfect. It was messy and confusing, and she didn't really know what to think after last night. But despite all of that, this was exactly where she wanted to be right now. With Erik.

Because the thing she'd been fighting for, the emotions she'd denied having to Ally, were burning inside her chest right now. She was in love with Erik. Larissa wanted not just him, but *this* life here. Where people knew each other and cared for one another. Growing up by herself with only minimal help or attention from her parents from a far too early age, she didn't know what it was like to have an entire village at her side. Not until now, when she'd met and treated and formed connections with all the people in Svalbard. With Erik.

He'd asked her to stay. To move into his cabin. Her heart had nearly burst out of her chest as he'd said it, chipping away at her last defences and bringing her face-to-face with her feelings for Erik.

But he'd asked her to stay. Had told her that

he *liked* seeing her entangled in his life. Somewhere between their time at the research centre and now, he had changed his mind. And she had changed hers, too.

Larissa would stay.

Because she'd been able to live her life exactly how she'd wanted. There was no hardship, no compromise. No attempts to change her. Things were different from the past, from Rachel.

Maybe now she could finally have it all.

'There, look at the horizon,' Erik said above her, and she shifted her eyes towards it. Erik had put a harness with light strips on Midnight and attached a long leash before letting her loose in the snow. She smiled as the dog jumped around in the snow, then focused back on the horizon.

The inky black was now a familiar sight, the stars so much brighter than she'd ever seen them in England. But slowly the darkness gave way, and a lighter blue mixed into the blackness. Larissa sat up as she noticed the gradual change, watching with wide eyes as for the first time in weeks, the sky changed colour—permitting a hint of a sunrise with the light blue haze covering the horizon.

When she turned to look up at Erik, his smile was broad and brilliant under the light of the stars. He was an amazing person, and she couldn't believe that chance had brought them together. Or that he felt the same way as she did.

'I thought you might like to see Svalbard's first official sunrise of the year.' He gestured towards the horizon.

Larissa smiled up at him, her chest so full she could hardly contain it. 'I'm keen to see what it's like when the sun comes up and never dips below the horizon.'

Erik tilted his head to the side, a fine line appearing between his brows. 'Are you planning to come back in a few months to see it?'

The warm glow in her chest winked out, letting the icy air surrounding them filter through her skin. 'No, I—' She paused, unsure what to say as her mind spun out of control. Because that question he'd asked made absolutely no sense. Of course she was going to be here. He'd *asked* her to…

'I thought I'd stay here. With you. Move in. That's what you said. To move in with you and stay here. Together.' Her voice strained against the words, suddenly fearful of saying them when just a few moments ago, the truth of her feelings for Erik had run so clearly through her. There was no way she had misinterpreted that moment.

He was leading her on.

Beside her, Erik stiffened, and when his arm

fell away from her shoulder, Larissa realised that somehow they hadn't meant the same thing at all.

'That's not... Larissa, why are you saying this? We had an agreement about what this could and couldn't be. You can't do this to me now.' His voice was rough and so unlike anything she'd heard from him in the past few weeks. Ice gathered around her stomach as she sensed Erik slipping out of her grasp—and with him the future she'd only dared to envision yesterday.

'Do this to you?' Her defences kicked in at his phrasing. '*You* started this. You said last night how much you enjoyed seeing me in your cottage—in your life. It was you who asked me to stay. I thought you were saying—' The rest of her words died in her throat as all breath left her lungs at his shocked expression.

'That's not what I said.' He paused, and she could see the internal debate flickering over his expression as he, too, replayed last night in his head. 'I invited you to stay with me because we only have two weeks left, and I thought we both wanted to make the most of this. I never meant...'

His voice trailed off, and Larissa was grateful for the silence. She pushed herself off the bench, bringing some physical distance between them. Strange how this was the thing she wanted both most and least in this situation.

He hadn't meant any of it.

The realisation hit her like a ton of bricks,

pushing any remaining vestiges of air out of her lungs. 'Oh my God, I feel so *stupid*. I was ready to let it all go, despite my growing feelings for you. I had convinced myself that it didn't matter and that I couldn't go back on my word. But then you showed up at my door, and you invited me over to your house. Not only that, but you told me you want me to stay, and dumb me thought you meant *forever.*'

Erik's gaze snapped to her, his eyes widening enough that she knew he had no idea about the depth of her feelings. So there was no way he reciprocated any of them. She was just some fun entertainment. Just like he said she would be. She should have believed him.

'Larissa, I'm sorry. This isn't—I couldn't…' His head drooped down, nervous fingers running through his still dishevelled hair. Hair she now knew to be so soft as it ran through her fingers. She wished she had never learned that, because missing him would be the hardest part about leaving.

'We haven't discussed forever. Didn't we both agree that this couldn't be anything more than that?' His voice wobbled. Or maybe Larissa just wished to hear that—to know that this was hard for him. 'I can't leave here.'

Larissa forced a breath down. 'I didn't ask you to leave, nor would I *ever* do that. Not after learning what happened to you and how you feel about Svalbard. You don't believe the people have grown on me, too?'

'I can't ask you to stay here. What if—'

She interrupted him. 'You're not asking. That's the whole point of this. I thought you were, but apparently that was all in my head. Our connection, our *emotions*. All made up.'

Erik surged to his feet. With one step he was halfway across to her, and his hands hovered in the air. But then they dropped back to his sides in tight fists. 'You'll change your mind. Living here is not as easy as you seem to think. You've been here six weeks. What makes you think you can even fathom what the rest of your life would be like here?'

She staggered back at his words. His lack of faith in her conviction… 'You don't believe I know what I'm doing? That I know my own mind?'

He shook his head. 'I just don't believe love can conquer all.'

She flinched at that, his words hitting her right in the chest. 'In that case, let me say that while I appreciate the offer, I won't stay with you in the cottage. I'm afraid my feelings for you run a lot deeper than you're comfortable with, and so it's best we stop this now.' She forced the words out of her tight throat, swallowing the emotions trying to escape her. This was the right thing to do, no matter how wrong it felt.

'Larissa, I don't know how we got here. Please, I...' The genuine hurt in his voice urged her to rush over to him, wrap her arms around him and pull him close. She pushed that urge away.

'Please take me back home. I think we said everything we needed to say.' Erik stared at her, his mouth set in an almost defiant frown. Internally, she willed him to take it all back, to tell her he felt the same way and they could figure things out.

Her heart shattered when he let out a sigh and nodded as he untied Midnight's leash and reeled her back in.

This wasn't how they were supposed to end. Yet here they were.

The next two weeks would be tricky. But there was no way she would abandon her posting here, no matter how much she hurt. Because even though her feelings revolved around Erik, the people of this place still needed her. She hadn't taken this responsibility lightly, and that he would even insinuate she did sliced far deeper than she'd expected.

Though how she would go about working the next two weeks without seeing him and deepening the wounds inside her, she had no clue. Larissa would just have to figure it out.

One day at a time.

CHAPTER ELEVEN

IT WAS DONE. Erik stared at the clock on his phone, then lifted the beer bottle to his lips and took a deep breath. Fragments of conversations from other patrons of the bar floated around him, but he didn't pay them any mind.

Her plane had officially left, and Larissa was out of his life forever. The two weeks he'd hoped to have—fourteen days he'd known would never be enough to satiate the need for her—had been cut short by her unexpected confession. And his hideous response to it. Just thinking about it sent a cringe through him, and he took another sip of his beer to chase the memory away.

He'd seen her at the hospital, going about her shifts like the professional he knew her to be, but somehow they had reached the silent agreement that they would stay out of each other's way. Or maybe the hurt he'd inflicted on her ran too deep for her to even see him. The problem was how badly he wanted to see her. How *desperately* he wanted to go back on his word and tell her the truth. Because the last two weeks had given him enough distance and perspective to understand how much Larissa had changed his life for the better.

And it was because of that knowledge that he couldn't let her stay here. Not when she might end up resenting him for making her move. What if she wasn't happy here? They would end up at the same intersection again, where they would each have to bend in ways they couldn't just to accommodate the other.

'I think that's the first time I've seen you in here,' a familiar voice said, and he looked up just in time to watch his sister plop down on the opposite chair.

'I could say the same thing,' he replied, though he knew that was because he rarely went out to any of the bars in town. Not unless one of his patients was celebrating something important or there was a community event.

'That's because *you're* never here.' Anna reached over to grab his bottle and took a sip. She shook as she set it down, scrunching up her face. 'Ah, this still tastes awful.'

'Then don't drink it,' he replied, rolling his eyes at his sister.

Anna didn't reply, but instead reached across the table and touched his phone to reveal the time.

She hummed as she tapped her finger against her cheek.

'What?'

'It's an unusual time for you to be here. It's not right after a shift at the hospital, which I think would be the natural time for you to be out.' She paused, levelling a stare at him that seemed vaguely familiar. It was the same look his mother had used on them growing up. Before he could say anything, she continued, 'Unless you wanted to be somewhere noisy and busy for a certain event. But what could that event be?'

Now it was his turn to level the same withering glare at her. 'If you have something to say, just come right out and say it.'

'You needed to be somewhere with people around you for when Larissa's flight departed.' There wasn't any smugness in her words like he'd expected, which had him looking up at her. Her expression was soft, as if she not only knew how he was feeling, but she also understood.

He said nothing to that. Didn't really know what to say. That he had let the woman he loved slip out of his grasp? That he flip-flopped between regret and emptiness whenever he thought about his life without her? Admitting that to himself was already far too much of a challenge. He couldn't possibly tell his sister. Even though she was sitting right there, urging him to go on.

'We got close during her time here. It shouldn't be surprising to feel something about her departure,' he said, hedging his words carefully.

By the frown appearing on his sister's face, he knew she wasn't going to let this go. 'I admit I've let you take the easy way out far too often. To the point where you don't really have to confront any of the tension around you.'

Erik bristled at that. 'The easy way out? I don't think—'

'I get that our parents can be overbearing, especially when a significant other is involved. Believe me, they never shut up about me finding someone and settling down, either. I get it. So when the whole thing with Astrid happened, I said nothing. I did nothing, either. That's probably on me.' Anna sighed as she shook her head, ignoring what Erik had been about to say. 'She wasn't good for you anyway, so I have limited regrets there. But with Larissa... You came to the hotel. *Unprompted.*'

He had. After avoiding the hotel ever since his breakup with Astrid two years ago, he had stopped going there because he had no reason to be there. They were too nosy, too obsessed with the next match that might come in and turn his life upside down. He just couldn't deal with the consistent comments, so he'd stopped going all together.

But when he'd come back from Norway after not seeing Larissa for a few days, he hadn't hesitated to seek her out at his parents' hotel. In fact, her whereabouts hadn't even factored into his thinking at all. He'd just wanted to see her.

Just like he wanted to see her now. Or any time of the day.

'She said she wants to move here,' he whispered on an exhale.

'I figured as much when she hardly left the hotel for her last fourteen days here. I also imagine you told her she couldn't possibly mean that and subsequently pushed her away.' She reached across the table again, and Erik looked up when she rested her hand on top of his clenched fist.

'She doesn't know what it means to live here. What she would give up.' That was at the heart of the problem. How could he accept her sacrifice when he knew she would come to regret it eventually?

'That's not really for you to decide,' Anna said, giving his hand a squeeze for emphasis.

Erik opened his mouth to protest, but the words died in his throat. He had no real argument for that. Or against that. Though he was loath to hear it, his sister had a point. Larissa had not only made the choice to come here in the first place, but she had also sought the company of the people in the village. Had even gone so far as to walk

Martin's dog when he couldn't. And during the incident with the polar bear, she hadn't needed any of his guidance. She'd known how to act because she had paid attention to the people around her and how to live a life on Svalbard.

'What if she regrets coming here? What if love isn't enough?' he said so quietly, Anna had to lean forward. The last fourteen days had been torture, and he was at the point where he had to admit to himself that Larissa owned his entire heart.

He loved her.

She squeezed his hand again and said, 'What if it is, though?'

Erik stilled at the question. It tripped up something inside him simply because he had never asked that question. All of his thoughts had revolved around the sacrifices she would have to make and the regret that would follow. That's how it had happened with Astrid. But had she ever really fit in the way Larissa had? He couldn't imagine Astrid ever offering to walk someone's dog.

'That's a lot riding on what-if,' Erik said, even as he felt himself slipping—let himself consider whether the what-if his sister posed could be true. What would life be like if Larissa was here with him, running the hospital and then going back home with him every night?

It would be the best version of his life he could

imagine. If she were to give him this gift—and she had—he would be foolish not to grasp it with both hands.

The clarity of his thoughts must have been easy to read, for a grin spread over Anna's face. 'You're a doctor *and* you grew up in this family. So you know that when things don't work out, you deal with it when it happens. You don't over-think what *could* happen in some hypothetical scenario. I'd hate for you to lose out on something great just because it *might* not work out.' She paused, withdrawing her hand from his. 'What happened with Astrid was messed up. I know that her leaving felt like you would never be able to have something like this again. But give Larissa some credit. She might know what she wants. Don't let a hypothetical get in the way of your own happiness.'

His own happiness? Was it absurd that until this point, he had never contemplated it? For the longest time, he'd believed that the ideas of his parents were the most important thing in his life, and when he'd defied their wishes, he'd felt it every single day. Then the only way of making this sacrifice worth it was to ensure he had done it for the greater good. To help his community.

Asking Larissa to stay here with him would only be for him. Because he loved her. She needed to know that, in case his actions hadn't made that clear. And of course they hadn't, because like the idiot he was, he'd pushed her away in fear of history repeating itself. But how could it when things were so fundamentally different? When he hadn't even hesitated to part ways with Astrid, but the thought of Larissa now being out of his reach squeezed all the air from his lungs?

Anna nodded as if she'd been following his thoughts. 'Great. Now that we sorted this out, I have a present for you.'

Erik furrowed his brow. A present? 'I don't have time for that. I need to figure out what to do about Larissa. I told her to leave, let her believe I didn't feel the same way about her.' What a foolish thing he'd done. He'd been wrapped up in his own drama and hadn't even seen what was clear in front of him—how much he loved Larissa and that his life would be so much less without her.

Would she even give him a chance to speak to her again? He couldn't fault her if she was done with him for good. Erik hadn't really left any wiggle room.

'Well, I happen to know that someone didn't check out this morning. It seems like she moved her flight to next week and booked another week at the hotel.' Anna smiled as she said that, then grabbed his beer bottle to take another sip that made her shudder in disgust.

'Wait... She's still here?' Was that what she

was trying to tell him? That Larissa hadn't left on the flight today? Erik was on his feet before he even had the chance to think differently.

'Go grovel and get her back. Going by all the ice cream containers in her bin, you'll need to do a lot of grovelling,' his sister said, but Erik was only half listening as he pocketed his phone and left the bar.

Some strange twist of fate had granted him one more chance to tell her how he felt. He would not let it slip through his fingers this time.

'Here is a suggestion—instead of watching another season of *The Great British Bake Off*, why don't you go talk to Thor and tell him you're not taking no for an answer?' Ally said with a surprisingly straight face.

Larissa looked into her half-empty tub of ice cream and then down at the oversized tee and equally large sweatpants she'd been living in for two days now. There were some clear advantages of being out of work, and not having to look presentable was definitely one of them.

'Mmm, pass,' she said as she speared her spoon into the tub once more to retrieve another mouthful of ice cream.

After their disastrous Valentine's Day date, Larissa had to keep it together and professional for an entire two weeks. Two weeks of seeing him at the hospital and wondering how she had got it so wrong. Though she knew she'd kept her cool at work, the pain following her around had been near overwhelming.

Ally sighed, hanging her head in defeat. 'Why not?'

'Because he basically told me to pack it and leave him alone,' Larissa said, pointing her smudged spoon at her best friend. Even in sub zero temperatures, ice cream remained the saddest and most calming of foods.

When Ally frowned, Larissa added, 'There is no other way to slice it, Ally. I told him I wanted to stay, and he said he didn't mean to suggest that, so I left. That was the sensible thing to do in this situation.'

'You're not supposed to do the sensible thing when in love. No, you do the crazy things, the scary things. The things that are living inside your heart and just about ready to burst.' Ally waved her arms around as she said that, painting an overdrawn picture that was almost enough to make Larissa smile and feel normal again.

Though she doubted she would ever fully feel like herself again. Not when Erik had forever rearranged things inside her. She'd come here convinced that her life would be about her work, about always watching love and connections unfold from the outside without ever getting to be

a part of it. Because her parents hadn't taught
her these skills, she would forever miss out on
them. Rachel had supplied her with proof that
she couldn't be with someone the way books and
movies had taught her, and now Erik... The way
she had misread his intentions just showed that
she couldn't do it.

Larissa was flawed, and there was no way out
of it.

'I know this face. Stop doom-spiralling and
thinking you are somehow broken inside. You are
not. People get it wrong all the time.' She paused
at the end of the sentence, and now it was Larissa's turn to roll her eyes.

'I'm just saying that I spent two months here
getting to know the locals through my work at the
hospital, and I've grown to like them. I thought
they'd grown to like me too, and it's bumming me
out that I was wrong about this.' Erik's rejection
had hit her far harder than she'd expected, and it
taught her again not to trust her heart.

'That's not accurate, though. Erik didn't say
that he loves you, but neither did you. So I don't
think you can really judge him on that. There is
no way a guy shows you the first sunrise of the
year and doesn't want it to be a romantic gesture.
But even if it's accurate, that doesn't mean everyone else rejected you, too.' Ally's stare bore
into her even through the screen and thousands

of kilometres between them. 'Hasn't Anna been supplying you with ice cream for two weeks? Does she know what went on between you two?'

She had. After coming home from the hospital one day, Larissa had found a mini-freezer next to her fridge and upon opening it had found it stacked up with different ice cream flavours that must have cost a fortune.

'I don't think so. Maybe? She saw us together at the hotel before Valentine's Day, but we weren't too obvious, I hope. She just knows I'm sad for some reason, and ice cream is the saddest food out there.'

Come to think of it, even though nobody *should* have known what happened between her and Erik, Anna hadn't been the only one to check in. Larissa knew that any kind of news in the community spread fast. However, because they'd never been a real couple, she'd thought no one would notice the tension between her and Erik.

But every day at work, Ingrid had checked in with her, sometimes even warning her of Erik's schedule and where he might be at certain times. Martin had also appeared at the hotel, offering her his and Storm's company if she wanted to go out.

Despite owing her no loyalty and only knowing her for two months, the community of Longyearbyen had shown up for her. Even through all the hurt, her heart squeezed at the thought, longing to remain a part of this. Except Erik didn't want her here.

'It doesn't matter. After what happened between us, there is no way I can just stay here. He's the head of the hospital I would need to work at, and I don't think he's well-inclined to hire me.' She paused, following the thoughts all the way to the end. This wasn't the first time in the last two weeks that Larissa had contemplated staying and wondered what would happen if she did. It scared her how much that thought enticed her.

So she quickly added, 'Plus, you're not here, and that's a non-negotiable for me.'

Ally shook her head. 'Oh no, no, no. Do not put this on me. I'm not letting you hide behind that flimsy excuse. We've made things work long-distance already. You're my ride or die, Larry. No amount of distance will ever change that.'

With her last excuse gone, Larissa had no choice but to look inward and confront the feelings that had been brewing for the last two weeks. She wanted to be with Erik far more than she could have ever expected when they'd started their fling. But even more, she felt a genuine connection to Longyearbyen and her place in it. She didn't want to leave, and a part of her had already known that when she'd moved her flight.

Leaving now, while everything had been un-

ravelling round her, had just been too much for
her. Because even though the fling with Erik
was over, something inside her balked at the
thought of leaving. At some point over the last
eight weeks, this town had become her home.
She couldn't just up and leave all of this behind,
could she?

But how could she consider staying when
her relationship with Erik was now so fraught?
Would it even be possible when her ability to
work hinged on him? He needed another doctor at
the hospital, and her placement with New Health
Frontiers showed he had trouble finding staff.

But did she really want to subject herself to
seeing him every day?

'So you think I should stay? Even though I
would have to work with my ex…something day
in and day out?' It sounded like the worst idea
she'd ever had, so why was her heart fluttering
at the idea?

'I can't tell you what to do, but I can say that
I've never seen you this involved outside of our
friendship. Even if you take Erik out of it, I've
seen a change in you. I think you'd be silly not to
explore it.' Ally shrugged. 'And even if it doesn't
end up working out, you can always come back.
What do you have to lose at this point?'

Larissa snorted at that because the answer was
clear—precious little. Her heart was already bat-

tered and bruised. What was one more round of that if it meant some closure for her?

She groaned as she pushed herself to her feet, stashing the half-eaten ice cream in her freezer. 'You're really annoying. I hope you know that,' she said with a grumble. But Ally was right. The deep sorrow she'd experienced in the last two weeks was connected to Erik, yes. But it was also connected to the people she'd met along the way and a sense of belonging almost foreign to her.

It was worth a fight, even if she got hurt all over again. If he told her to get lost, she would accept it—but she would tell him she planned on staying with or without him. This had become her home, too.

'So what are you going to do now?' Ally asked, sitting up straight.

'I'm going to go talk to him. Because you're bullying me to do that. I would be happy to just come back and forget this ever happened, but you need me to go through some personal growth.'

Ally laughed at that, the sound burrowing through her chest and straight into her heart— filling her with a glowing warmth. 'I'm proud of you, Larry. I know something great is waiting for you down that road, even if it is a struggle to get there.'

Larissa swallowed the tightness building in her throat, then said her goodbyes to Ally after getting dressed and getting the okay from her best friend that she looked presentable enough to confront the man she was in love with one last time.

When she picked up the phone and opened his message thread to send him a text, she froze in place. A new message from him had appeared.

Erik: I'm coming over. Please open the door. I need to talk to you before you leave.

Her heart beat in her throat as she read those words and absorbed the urgency in them. Her fingers hovered over the keyboard on the phone screen, trying to squeeze the right words out of her brain. Was he coming to see her off? To tell her he'd made a mistake? Or did he somehow know she wanted to stay, and he was coming over to stake a claim on Svalbard?

She'd typed out, I'm still at the hotel. Are you—when a knock sounded on her door. She almost dropped her phone as her heart leapt into her throat.

Hand shaking, she reached for the handle and pulled the door open. Erik stood in the doorframe, as tall and handsome as she remembered him. Her heart ached for her to reach out and touch him. Sink into the touch she had not felt in so long.

'I didn't leave.' She blurted out the first words coming to her mind and then cringed when she heard them. Of course she hadn't left. She was standing right here in front of him.

'I know,' he said with a lopsided grin, and some of the tension eased out of her at the pearly flash of teeth. He was smiling. Not as brightly as he used to, but he *was* smiling.

'Funny thing, I was about to text you when your message came up.' His eyebrows shot up at her words, his head tilting to the side enough that the top of his head brushed against the doorframe. The smile he flashed her was tentative, and she had to resist being sucked into his orbit straight away. She needed to talk to him first.

'I'm considering staying here. On Svalbard.' Surprise rippled over his face when she added, 'For good.'

'Is that why you didn't fly out today? You want to stay?' Larissa stilled at that. He knew her flight would have been today?

'I… No. Or maybe yes. I don't know.' His eyes were alight with a familiar spark, and she took a step back as his gaze threatened to undo her composure. 'My feelings about you haven't changed, but what I realised in the last two weeks is that I built something here. Something that I cherish. I want to share this with you, I really do. But I need you to know that I'm staying, no matter what.'

Larissa let out a deep breath as the words flowed out of her and she told him what she

needed him to know. What she hadn't understood two weeks ago when everything happened.
Erik was a big part of why this place had become
her home, and her heart would ache if he didn't
choose her. But he had to understand that his
choice wasn't between her and his community.
Regardless, she wasn't going anywhere.

Erik's expression slackened, and the lightness
in his eyes—the spark of vulnerability—made
her knees weak. Her eyes dipped down to his
throat as he swallowed. His chest heaved as he
took a deep breath and released it in a measured
exhale.

'I owe you an apology, Larissa. I freaked out.
Hard. Because I've never had someone be this
important to me.' He paused to take another
breath. 'I pushed you away because when you
said you couldn't wait to see the midnight sun
with me, I could picture it. With every blink, the
image of you being here forever formed in my
mind, burned itself into my heart. But I... I've
been in this moment before, and I was scared that
this time I wouldn't survive losing the woman I
love if I let myself sink into this relationship too
deep.'

Larissa's breath caught in her throat. 'The
woman you love?' Had he really just said those
words?

He let out a thin laugh. 'Yeah, something I

should have had the courage to say sooner. I love you, Larissa. When we were in bed and I was watching you slowly wake up, I thought I wanted to see this happen a thousand times over. Wanted to learn all the different ways you can wake up. It hit at that moment that if you asked me for something—*anything*—I would have done everything within my power to give it to you. That scared me to my bones, and so when you said you wanted to stay, I panicked.'

Erik lifted his hand but stopped just before he touched her. 'Please forgive me. I've been living alone for a long time, and I won't always know the right way to go about things. But I want to try. For you, I want to learn.' He let out a huff of laughter. 'I came here to tell you we can figure this out. As long as you take me back, I don't care how we do things. Because I love you, and I want you in my life in whatever form you're willing to give me.'

Larissa had stopped breathing halfway through his speech, and only as he finished did she remember to fill her lungs with air. 'I was crushed and thought about leaving immediately. After what happened with Rachel, I thought I would never let myself feel this way again. The risks were just not worth it. But you somehow slipped in, right under my skin.'

She brushed her hand over her arm, tracing

over her skin as she paused, casting her eyes down as she searched for the right words. 'I don't want to repeat mistakes either. And maybe I did by making assumptions about your intentions without bringing it up. I heard what I wanted to hear and just ran with it. What is different now from where we both were before we met?'

'We are different. What *we* have is different. Unique.' His voice dropped low, sliding over her skin and through her pores. The air grew thick around them as he stepped close enough that she could count his eyelashes. 'I haven't felt this way about anyone, ever. And yes, it's mad, but I *know* I need you in my life, however you are willing to let me be in yours.'

Her throat was thick, and words refused to form in her voice box. So instead, she reached out to where his hand hovered in the air between them and took it into hers. Then she pulled him closer, over the threshold of her room and into her arms. 'I love you, Erik. And I'll make sure that we *are* different. Because you showed me things I didn't realise I could feel. This place.' She lifted her hand, indicating where they were but also so much beyond. 'This place taught me belonging on a level I've never experienced before. I want to be a part of this because it's already become a part of me.'

His shoulders slumped, and his weight sagged

against her in a relief that was too stark for words. Not that they needed words when they had their hands and bodies and lips to express what they couldn't otherwise.

Larissa sighed when his arms came around her, pressing her close to him. She breathed in his scent and knew she had found what she hadn't realised she'd been looking for all this time.

'I'm home,' she whispered into his neck as he held her tight, and hoped this moment would last forever.

* * * * *

*Look out for the next story in the
Valentine Flings duet*

Nurse's Keralan Temptation
by Becky Wicks

*And if you enjoyed this story, check out these
other great reads from Luana DaRosa*

Pregnancy Surprise with the Greek Surgeon
Surgeon's Brooding Brazilian Rival
A Therapy Pup to Reunite Them

All available now!